Sky Races

Welcome to "Sky Races," the exhilarating sequel to "Journey to the Sky." In this thrilling continuation, the spirit of adventure soars to new heights as we delve into the dynamic world of competitive airship racing.

Our hero, Jedidiah Davenport, returns with his unyielding determination and innovative spirit. This time, he faces even higher stakes. Having conquered the challenges of the rugged American West, Jedidiah now turns his eyes to the skies, ready to take on a new frontier filled with daring rivals and technological marvels.

Set against an expansive racecourse that spans continents, "Sky Races" blends the raw excitement of high-speed competition with the rich, imaginative world of Steampunk. The race is not just a test of speed but ingenuity and bravery, with competitors navigating through cities, across oceans, and over mountains.

In this gripping tale, Jedidiah is joined by familiar faces and new allies. Phineas B. Hargroves, with his eccentric genius, continues to push the boundaries of invention, while new adversaries emerge, each coveting the title of the sky's fastest. The enigmatic Myra Wilhelmina Bancroft presents a formidable challenge, her prowess and cunning rivaling even Jedidiah's own.

"Sky Races" immerses you in a vivid world filled with steampunk wonders—airships, innovative machinery, and other anachronistic technologies that infuse the story with a sense of wonder and possibility. The narrative is rich with the sights, sounds, and sensations of a world in flux, where the industrial age collides with the boundless imagination of human ingenuity.

This novel is more than a tale of high-flying adventure. It's a story of resilience, friendship, and the relentless pursuit of dreams. Jedidiah's journey through the skies challenges him to confront not only his competitors but also his own fears and limitations.

Prepare to be swept off your feet and into the clouds, where every twist and turn brings new excitement and discovery. The sky is not the limit—it's just the beginning.

Sitting on the deck of the unknown airship,
ready to be used against them, was the
Ultrasonic Disruptor Cannon.

Sky Races

A Jedidiah Davenport Adventure

BY PAUL EDWARD TURNER

Contents

CHAPTER I

Founder's Day Fiasco

A sudden gunshot rang through the air, making Jedidiah Davenport's heart beat rapidly against his chest. He quickly spurred his horse forward, prompting Blaze to burst into a gallop. Jedidiah tuned out the dozens of men on horseback galloping behind him and focused on the path ahead. The scent of dust and earth filled his nostrils, mixing with the faint smell of sweat and leather from his faithful steed.

Gravel and dirt flew beneath the thundering hooves as Jedidiah leaned low in his saddle, pushing for more speed. The shouts of the men echoed, urging their horses to close the gap, their presence an ever-growing threat at his back. The path ahead twisted through the wild terrain, the wind whipping against his face and tugging at his hat. Jedidiah navigated each turn with practiced precision, his body moving in perfect sync with his

Jedidiah Davenport galloped through
the wild terrain on his horse, Blaze,
with unwavering determination.

horse.

Every muscle tensed, ready for the slightest sign of trouble. His eyes darted to the treeline, half-expecting a rifle's crack or a lasso's whip at any moment. The valley opened up before him, the vast expanse a daunting stretch to freedom. With a sharp whistle, he commanded more speed from his mount. The steady rhythm beneath him was the only reassurance he felt.

Only when he thundered past the old oak tree, the unofficial marker of safety, did the realization begin to sink in. The familiar sounds of the crowd's cheers grew from a distant rumble to a deafening roar. His heart still pounded, a wild drumbeat in his chest, but now with exhilaration, not fear. As the finish line came into view, framed by fluttering flags and vibrant banners, the thrill of the Spoon Fork Annual Horse Race was pulsing through his veins.

Just as the young man was confident he would cross the finish line first, he caught a glimpse of his foreman, Jim Davis, riding hard and coming up on his left side. To his right was Jacob Harrington, the town blacksmith. It was a close race, but Jim Davis managed to edge his employer out by a nose. Jedidiah came in second, and Jacob Harrington came in third. They were followed closely by Matthew Colton and the rest of the men who had entered the race.

As the crowd erupted into a mix of applause and a few disappointed groans, Jedidiah eased his horse to a trot, the animal's sides heaving from the exertion. The continuous shouts and cheers of the fairground filled the air and blended into a harmonious celebration. Jim Davis, a grin wide on his face, tipped his hat to Jedidiah, who returned the gesture with a good-natured nod. "Next time, Jed!" Jim called out, his voice tinged with friendly competition.

Jedidiah couldn't help but chuckle. "You just wait until next year," he promised, his competitive spirit undimmed by the narrow loss.

The blacksmith, Jacob Harrington, reined in beside them, his chestnut mare blowing hard. "I thought I had you both for a moment," he said, his smile betraying no hint of his earlier determination to win.

Matthew Colton pulled up, the dust settling around his boots as he dismounted. "Gosh, that was a swell race," he commented, clapping Jedidiah on the back.

Adrenaline still coursed through Jedidiah's veins as he patted his horse, savoring the moment. The roar of the crowd softened into a gentle hum as they slowly began to disperse. Some lingered to exchange stories of past races, while others turned their attention to the refreshment tents. Jedidiah watched as children darted between the legs of adults, their laughter mingling with the residual excitement in the air. He took a deep breath.

The Founder's Day festival was a momentary escape from the mundane life of Spoon Fork. But as his gaze shifted to the horizon, where the silhouette of an airship cast a long shadow as it descended toward the fairground, he knew that the true test of his courage lay in the skies. His friend and eccentric mentor, Phineas B. Hargroves, hovered above him in his ship, the Icarus.

Phineas was using his newest invention, a camera with a long-distance telescopic lens for taking close-ups. It also featured a high speed shutter borrowed from an idea he saw in California. He aimed to capture some spectacular images of the race from above.

Jedidiah's thoughts suddenly turned to his freight company. With his former office manager, Charles Clayton, behind bars, his childhood friend, Matthew Colton, had been placed in charge of the main branch.

Matthew had been in this position for the past three months, immediately following the incident involving Elijah Perkins and the Railroad. Davenport felt fortunate to have such a loyal friend he could depend on.

Back in his present thoughts, Jedidiah continued patting his horse on the neck, whispering words of praise. Tom Miller, the young man who had helped bring Clayton and Perkins to justice, came walking over and offered to take care of the animal for him.

"Thanks, Tom," Jedidiah smiled appreciatively. "That's very kind of you."

"No problem, Mr. Davenport!" The younger man was honored to do it.

"Tom," Jedidiah chuckled as he shook his head. "I told you before, call me Jed."

"Oh yeah," Tom replied, flustered. "I'm sorry, Mr. Daven… I mean Mr… I mean Jed!" He turned on his heel and started to lead Blaze away, as the stallion was more than ready for a cool-down after the race.

"And don't forget to stop by our tent! Pat has made some of the best vittles you've ever tasted!" Jedidiah called after him.

"Sure thing, Jed," Tom called back, his voice trailing off as he continued walking. The young man couldn't help but feel a swell of pride working for someone like Jedidiah Davenport, who, despite not winning the race, still wore a winner's smile.

As Jedidiah turned to rejoin the remnants of the crowd, he was approached by Sheriff Thompson.

"Enjoying the festivities, Sheriff?" Jedidiah asked with a raised eyebrow, noting the man's solemn expression.

"More or less," Thompson replied, his gaze scanning the crowd. "Just keeping an eye out for trouble, especially with so many folks gathered in one place."

Jedidiah nodded, understanding his concerns. "Never a dull moment, huh?"

Thompson chuckled softly but then turned serious. "Got a minute? There's something I need to talk to you about."

Jedidiah's pulse quickened, sensing that the day's excitement was far from over. "Of course, Sheriff. What's on your mind?"

Thompson glanced around, making sure no one was close by. "It's about that airship race coming up. I've been hearing some talk that not everyone's planning to play fair."

Jedidiah's face hardened slightly at the news. He glanced up at the Icarus and then back at the sheriff. "What kind of talk?"

"There's been rumors about heavy bets being placed," Thompson explained, lowering his voice. "With the race just a couple of weeks away, I'm concerned there might be some trouble. Folks are saying your friend Phineas and that Bancroft woman are the favorites."

"I take it nobody's betting on me," Jedidiah smiled cunningly.

"You've entered the race?" the sheriff's eyes showed clear signs of surprise. "I didn't know that. In that case, Jed, I really think you need to be careful."

"The race is miles away," Jedidiah remarked.

"The starting line is in Wichita and the checkpoints are in places like New York, Toronto, London, and Paris. The finish line is back where it started in Wichita."

"It doesn't matter where the race starts or ends," Sheriff Thompson interrupted. "The rumors are around here and it's my job to take them seriously. I would think you would be too, especially since you're going to be competing."

This time Jedidiah glanced around, ensuring their conversation remained private. "Perhaps you should keep that part under your hat. I haven't told anyone except Matt and Phineas. Everyone else thinks Matthew and I are just going to support the Professor. They don't know I'm racing."

"You know you can trust me not to say a word, Jed." Sheriff Thompson replied. "Just promise me you'll be careful."

Jedidiah acknowledged the older man's concern with a nod. "Don't worry, Sheriff," he assured him, "I'm as cautious as I am competitive. And with friends like Matt and Phineas, I've got the best lookout team anyone could ask for."

With a last glance at the hovering airship, Jedidiah turned to rejoin the others. His gaze caught the lively scene at the refreshment tent, where Pat Bennington, Jedidiah's personal cook, stood beaming as people from all around praised his food.

A young man, not much older than Tom, lingered at the outskirts of the tent, his attention split between the food and the intricate details of the nearby model airships on display. Something about the young man's demeanor caught Jedidiah's attention. The way his eyes seemed to assess rather than enjoy, calculating each detail with a sharpness that contradicted his casual stance. Jedidiah made a mental note to keep an eye on him.

Jim Davis, a man not prone to frivolity, approached Jedidiah with a subtle urgency in his stride. "Jed, I need to talk to you," the ranch foreman said quietly, "I've been hearing some rumors about the upcoming airship race."

"You too?" Jedidiah Davenport sighed.

"What do you mean?" Jim asked, puzzled.

"Nothing," Jedidiah replied, "it's just that rumors have a way of spreading fast in this town."

"You've already heard?"

"I get around," the young man smiled. Noticing the stern expression on the taller man's face, he added, "Look I'm sure it's nothing to be concerned about but let's keep our ears to the ground and not let speculations ruin the festival for us."

As the two men spoke, the figure at the edge of the tent shifted, his gaze sharpening at the mention of the sky race. Before anyone noticed his eavesdropping, he quietly took a few steps backward and disappeared into the crowd.

After finishing his talk with his foreman, Jedidiah Davenport walked over to the table displaying his miniature airships. Next to the scaled-down model of the Icarus stood one of his pride and joy, the Phoenix. Alongside these were three other nearly identical ships, with only slight modifications from their real-life counterparts. The Navigator, the Eclipse, and the Drifter. They were the newest additions to Jedidiah's growing fleet.

With the added wealth from the oil recently discovered on his land, Davenport had been able to expand his workforce and increase production. He had been constructing an average of one airship a month.

As the young man studied the models, a sense of pride washed over him. The Phoenix, in particular, was more than just an airship. It represented the culmination of Jedidiah's vision, a vessel as fierce and enduring as its namesake. He ran his fingers over the meticulously crafted replica, each curve and line a promise of the adventures to come.

The chatter around him faded into a buzz as he lost himself in thoughts of the approaching sky race. Jedidiah was no stranger to challenges, having faced down industrial giants and outlaws alike. Yet, this was a different beast altogether — a test of courage, determination, ingenuity, and strategy against the best the world had to offer.

"Speculation or not, we'll be ready," Jedidiah muttered under his breath, his gaze lifting to the Icarus. Phineas was still circling the festival, the bright morning sun glinting off his camera lens.

For now, however, Jedidiah decided to embrace the festival and savor the moment. After all, it was times like these that made all the hard work worthwhile. He headed inside the tent, drawn by the delicious aroma of Pat's cooking.

"Fix a plate for me!" Jedidiah called out, his voice carrying over the noise. With a hearty laugh, Pat turned from his bustling stove and gave him the high sign.

As Jedidiah was waiting, he mingled with other guests, inviting them all to come out to the ranch later that day for an after party. Just as he was about to reach for his plate, a sudden commotion broke the tranquil atmosphere.

Screams erupted from outside, cutting through the merriment like a knife. Jedidiah's heart pounded as he turned towards the source of the disturbance. His instincts took over, and he raced out to see what was happening. People were shouting, pointing towards the sky, their faces pale with fear.

The Icarus had floated down close enough for everyone to see Phineas B. Hargroves grappling with a large burly man on the deck of his ship. The sight was shocking, and the crowd was gasping.

Phineas struggled desperately, his hands

clutching at the man's arms, trying to break free. The burly man's face was twisted in anger as he shoved Phineas toward the railing. With a sudden, violent push, the eccentric older man lost his balance.

"Phineas!" Jedidiah shouted, his voice drowned out by the collective gasp of the crowd.

Time seemed to slow as Phineas teetered on the brink, his arms flailing as he tried to grab hold of something—anything—to stop his fall. But there was nothing. With a final, desperate look, Phineas toppled backward over the side of his ship, plunging headfirst toward the ground!

CHAPTER II

A Daring Rescue

Cries of terror pierced the air, and Jedidiah's heart once again began to beat against his chest. He pushed through the throng, his eyes locked on the horrifying sight of Phineas' body spiraling downward from the Icarus. Then, suddenly, the eccentric older man stopped falling. He was somehow hovering upside down several feet below his airship.

"How is that possible?" Jedidiah stood for a moment in disbelief. Suddenly remembering the goggles resting on the brim of his cap, he lowered them over his eyes and adjusted the lenses. The scene snapped into focus. Now, he could see how the famed inventor had performed this supernatural feat. Phineas' right foot was entangled in the rope ladder dangling from the side of his vessel.

"Jed!" Matthew Colton shouted as he arrived, breathless. "Phineas is..."

"I know!" Jedidiah interrupted, his gaze still locked above. "He's caught in the ladder. That's the only thing keeping him from falling. We've got to figure out a way to get him down!"

"What if you hovered your airship above his and dropped down on the airbag like you did when Elijah Perkins was holding him at gunpoint?" Matthew quickly suggested.

Jedidiah's mind flashed back to the event like it was yesterday. He remembered both the fear and the adrenaline from performing such a death-defying feat. The thought of repeating that maneuver once more sent chills down his spine. "That's one possibility," he mused, "but the Phoenix is back at the ranch, and my other airships are in service miles from here."

Scanning the area for anything that might cushion Phineas's landing, Jedidiah's eyes landed on the festival's quilting booth. They had a display of large, thick quilts that could possibly break the fall. Without another word, he and several quick-thinking bystanders grabbed one of the quilts and stretched it out below the older man.

The tension in the air was thick as Phineas continued to hang perilously from the side of the Icarus. Everyone held their breath, gripping the edges of the quilt, preparing for the outcome.

It was at this moment that Jedidiah spotted something that terrified him. Through his telescopic lenses, he witnessed the man Phineas had been tussling with lean over the railing, preparing to cut the ladder, with a large knife.

Just when Jedidiah thought this could be the end of his trusted mentor, a dark shadow suddenly engulfed him and the throng of people around him. Turning, he saw a second airship coming into view. It wasn't one of his fleet and didn't bear the signature style of any of Phineas' designs.

"Who is that?" Matthew cried out. "I've never seen that ship before!"

"It's the Enigma!" Jedidiah shouted, still looking through his goggles.

"The Enigma?" Matthew Colton repeated. "That's Myra Wilhelmina Bancroft's ship!"

On the deck of the sleek, dark-hulled airship stood a vision of audacious elegance and determination. She wore a white blouse with billowing sleeves cinched at the wrists with dark leather gloves. Over the blouse, she wore a vest fitted with various tools and gadgets, emphasizing her readiness for any situation. Her hair, meticulously styled in waves and curls, was held back by a pair of aviator goggles resting securely on her head, their lenses glinting in the sunlight.

Her sturdy trousers and knee-high boots suggested practicality and preparation for action. The revolver at her side and her look of confidence completed the image of a formidable and fearless adventurer.

"Gosh!" Matthew exclaimed. "Where did she come from?"

Before Jedidiah could respond, several gunshots rang through the air as Myra began firing at Phineas' assailant. The large burly man immediately stopped what he was doing and retreated from the railing. Myra then aimed what appeared to be a harpoon gun at the ship and fired. The spear stuck in the wall of the sleeper cabin, and the taut rope attached to the end successfully tethered the two ships together.

The adventurous woman wasted no time in securing a rugged leather harness around her torso. She then expertly attached a sturdy metal loop to the rope. With a confident check of her gear, she leaped over the railing and began sliding across. Moments later, she landed on the deck of the Icarus.

Upon sight, the large burly man began rushing towards her. In one quick motion, she unfastened her harness and rolled to safety. In what felt like the blink of an eye, the adventurous captain of the Enigma drew her revolver and was aiming it at her would-be assailant. "Don't try it!" she shouted.

Having no other choice, the large man did as instructed and stopped his advancement. "As you say," he snarled.

The older woman immediately began assessing

Myra aimed what appeared to be
a harpoon gun at the ship and fired.

the area and spotted a pulley system attached to the framework of the airship. This was part of Phineas's own design for lifting heavy cargo on and off the ship.

Without hesitation, Myra lunged toward it, her eyes scanning the mechanism. She turned and shouted to her would-be attacker, "Don't just stand there! Help me with this! We can use it to save Phineas." Reluctantly the large man did as instructed.

As Myra explained her plan, the burly man nodded, admittedly impressed by her quick thinking. He grabbed the free end of the rope and tied it into a loop that he lowered over the side of the ship.

"Phineas!" Myra shouted. "Slip that around your waist and we'll pull you up!"

Despite being upside down and dangling precariously from the side of his ship, Phineas managed to get the loop around his waist, his hands trembling the entire time. Myra directed the large man to start pulling.

The crowd held their breath as the pulley system groaned and creaked under the strain but held fast. Inch by inch, Phineas was lifted higher. Suddenly, the rope slipped from his waist, sliding up his legs. The tension was thick as the loop tightened around his ankles and miraculously held.

Cheers erupted from the relieved onlookers as

the eccentric older man was finally hoisted over the railing. Myra allowed herself a brief smile, though her eyes remained fixed on the assailant. She stood tall, her posture exuding confidence and control.

"Looks like it was a good thing for you that I came along when I did!" she called out, her voice cutting through the noise with a tone of authority.

"Good thing you came along!" Hargroves shouted, his voice dripping with sarcasm. Dangling upside down, he twisted and turned, struggling to look at her directly.

"Glad you agree with me for once in your life!" she replied, a smirk playing on her lips. She crossed her arms and leaned slightly to one side, conveying a mix of amusement and exasperation. "You'd probably be on the ground right now, while all the king's men tried to put you back together."

"Madam, I'll have you know I didn't need your help," the eccentric man protested, exaggeratedly waving his arms. "I was just biding my time, lulling that lowbrow brute into a false sense of security. At any moment, I was going to spring into action and execute my plan!"

"Before or after you plummeted to the ground?" Myra pointed towards the rope ladder still tangled around his leg. It was barely held together by a thread! Her eyebrow arched, and she leaned forward slightly to emphasize her point.

"You always have to make a grand appearance

and one-up me, don't you?" he fumed, his face reddening further with frustration. He flailed his arms in exasperation, trying to make his point despite his precarious position.

"You always have to complain every time I save your miserable hide, don't you?" she countered, her hands resting on her hips. She tilted her head slightly, clearly annoyed.

"Madam, I insist I didn't need your help!" Phineas's voice wavered, and for a moment Myra thought she saw a flicker of doubt in his eyes.

Myra Bancroft began glancing at the cabin door across from her and asked, "You still keep that pair of handcuffs in the top drawer?" She moved towards the cabin with purposeful strides.

"Where else would I keep them?" Phineas huffed, crossing his arms defensively as much as his position allowed.

The adventurous woman chose not to respond as she grabbed the key hanging on a peg outside the door and unlocked it. She motioned for her prisoner to step inside the room. Myra pointed towards the drawer in question and said, "Reach in there, put them on, and then toss me the key!"

After closing the door and locking him inside, she dropped both keys onto the deck of the ship directly below Phineas. Without saying a word, she turned and headed to the controls. A moment later, the Icarus was gaining altitude and floating above her ship, the Enigma.

"Madam, what are you doing?" the eccentric older man asked with disdain in his voice, his eyebrows furrowing in confusion.

"If you must know," she replied while reattaching the leather harness around her waist, her movements precise and unhurried. "I'm going back to my ship." She reached down and picked up the knife the man had used to cut the ladder. Myra stuck it into the wall within reach of the eccentric older man. "You can cut yourself down!" She huffed while reattaching the metal loop to the rope and beginning her return trip.

"Madam!" Phineas shouted. "Madam, wait!" Hargroves tried in vain to stop her, reaching out with one hand while the other clung to the rope, but it was too late and she was gone. He grumbled while struggling to reach the knife but still hanging upside down made it a bit of a challenge. His movements were awkward and clumsy as he twisted and turned.

"*You haven't changed a bit, have you, Myra?*" he thought to himself, as he stretched his arm for the blade. Finally, after several attempts, he managed to retrieve it and cut himself free.

"Ouch!" he shouted as he landed on the deck of his ship, rubbing his head and then his sore ankles and glaring in the direction of the Enigma.

On the ground below, Jedidiah continued

watching the scene the best he could. Most of the action had taken place out of his view but after seeing Myra Wilhelmina Bancroft retreating to her ship and cutting the rope that tethered the two vessels together he breathed a sigh of relief.

Minutes later, both airships began to descend and come to a resting spot in an open field not far from the festival. The crowds rushed to the area, everyone surrounding the Enigma to meet the daring and courageous woman who had just saved Hargroves' life.

Amidst applause and cheers, Myra disembarked from her airship with the poise and calm of a seasoned captain, nodding in acknowledgment of the crowd's admiration but keeping her emotions well under control.

Meanwhile, Phineas Hargroves, now safely on the ground but still visibly flustered from his ordeal, dusted off his clothes and tried to regain some semblance of dignity. His landing had been less than graceful, and he was keenly aware of the many eyes watching his every move.

"Thank you, everyone, for your concern," he announced to the gathered crowd, trying to mask his irritation with a forced smile. "However, I can assure you I was never in any danger and I could have handled the entire situation completely on my own."

"Guess I should have left you dangling in the air

since you obviously didn't my help!" Myra shot back, stepping closer and placing her hands on her hips.

The crowd turned their attention back to the adventurous airship captain as she started to make her way through the throng.

Jedidiah, who had been watching from a distance, approached her with a look of relief and respect. "That was impressive, Miss Bancroft. You handled that situation remarkably well."

Myra stopped and looked at Jedidiah, her eyes sharp yet not without warmth. "That's Ms. not Miss," she corrected him. "But thank you, and your name was?"

"Jedidiah," he responded. "Jedidiah Davenport."

The adventurous woman smiled and asked, "*The* Jedidiah Davenport?" She seemed quite impressed.

Jedidiah blushed and laughed nervously as he said, "I don't know of any others."

"In that case, Jed," she replied, "you can call me Myra."

Davenport felt quite honored by this and thanked her profusely. "It's a good thing you came along when you did Miss... Ms... Myra..." he stumbled over his words much the way Tom Miller had earlier with him. "Or it would have probably been the end of Professor Hargroves!"

Phineas turned sharply towards Jedidiah. "My

dear boy, I had matters completely under control!" He crossed his arms defensively, his face reddening with frustration. Due to the excitement and noise of the crowd, his words fell on deaf ears as nobody paid him any attention.

"It's nothing you wouldn't have done yourself," the adventurous woman replied modestly. "I read in the paper about how you saved his life a few months ago."

"I just did what had to be done," Jedidiah smiled. He turned and spotted the foreman of his ranch standing nearby. "If anyone deserves a round of applause, it's Jim Davis. He pulled Phineas out from a pile of timber when an unfinished section of my airship collapsed on top of him."

Jim nodded in appreciation but quickly deflected the attention from himself. "I'd say the real hero was the doctor who saved the Professor's life the time he got shot in the alley."

Phineas grew more agitated by the moment. He didn't appreciate the negative attention, and to make matters worse, Jedidiah's cook, Pat Bennington, was standing close by. The rotund man howled with glee as he elbowed the eccentric older man in the ribs. "Gosh, Hargy, I never realized how often you needed saving and rescuing!"

Trying to hold back his outrage, Phineas replied, "That's Hargroves, you dunderhead!"

Pat seemed unfazed by this outburst and

continued laughing. "Sorry, didn't realize how many times you needed saving and rescuing, *Hargroves*!" Before the inventor could reply, the cook turned back to the others and said, "Jed, Don't forget the time you saved him in Wichita after he got ambushed in his hotel room!"

"That's true, I..." Jedidiah suddenly spotted the expression on the older man's face and realized it would be best to change the subject. "Was there any damage to your ship in all the commotion?" he asked.

Phineas took a deep breath trying to release his frustration, "Nothing that can't be repaired." He turned on his heel and motioned towards the Icarus. "However, that scoundrel is still on board and I think he should be turned over to the authorities. He's still locked inside my cabin."

In the excitement of the rescue, everyone had completely forgotten about the large burly man who was responsible for everything.

"Quick, somebody find Sheriff Thompson!" Jedidiah exclaimed. He turned to his friend Matthew Colton. "Matt, he's around here somewhere. Go look for him!"

The young man turned and pushed his way through the crowd but didn't have to go far as he ran headfirst into the stern figure of the law.

"I heard, boy, and I saw everything!" Thompson declared as he made his way over to Jedidiah and the others. "Somebody go find my deputies!" He shouted. This time Jim Davis went for help while Matthew Colton stayed behind.

Upon reaching the airship, the Sheriff led the way up the ramp. Phineas unlocked the cabin door, and Sheriff Thompson, shotgun in hand, slowly turned the knob and stepped inside. He immediately turned back, puzzled. "Where is he?" he asked.

Phineas stepped forward, with a look of annoyance. "What do you mean, 'Where is he?' He's..." His jaw dropped as he looked inside. "He's gone!"

CHAPTER III

Back at the Ranch

"What do you mean, he's gone?" Myra Wilhelmina Bancroft asked as she pushed her way into the room. Much to her surprise, the large, burly man was nowhere to be seen.

"He must have gone through that window!" Jedidiah exclaimed, pointing to the shattered pieces of glass on the floor.

"The noise of the festival most likely masked the sound of his escape," Phineas B. Hargroves surmised.

"We'll search the grounds," Thompson said, motioning to his deputies. "Follow me, and keep your eyes open. He couldn't have gone far." The deputies nodded and swiftly exited the room.

After they had gone, Jedidiah scanned the area, his mind racing with thoughts of the escaped man. Turning to Myra, he managed a wry smile. "I don't suppose this was quite the arrival you were expecting."

"Not quite," she laughed, "but don't worry. I'm no stranger to excitement!"

The young entrepreneur realized what she meant. He had read every book, news article, and dime-store novel ever written about her. Myra Wilhelmina Bancroft had led one of the most exciting lives imaginable. Not only had she built her own airship, but she had also piloted it on many thrilling adventures. For example, on more than one occasion, Myra had faced down bands of sky pirates—something Jedidiah would experience in the not-too-distant future.

"I would love to hear more about your travels, Ms. Ban... Myra," Davenport corrected himself and then asked, "How would you like to visit my ranch this evening after the festival? A lot of the townspeople will be there."

Phineas B. Hargroves, overhearing the invitation, turned sharply toward Jedidiah. "My dear boy, I'm sure Myra has more important things to do than attending one of your dinner parties," he remarked.

Myra, clearly not used to having others speak for her, turned and looked directly at Phineas. "Actually, my evening is completely open. I would love to attend!" She felt a twinge of satisfaction at seeing Phineas' surprise.

"Well, that settles it!" Jedidiah smiled and

nodded. "I'll give you the coordinates to my ranch. There's an open field next to the hangars where Phineas and I store our airships. You can land there, and one of my men can bring you to the house in one of my buggies."

"Say, if Ms. Bancroft is gonna be there, this is gonna be the best party ever!" Matthew Colton suddenly exclaimed. By now, only he, Jedidiah, Myra, and Phineas remained aboard the Icarus. Everyone else had already gone back to the Founder's Day event. He turned to Phineas and asked, "What do you think?"

"I think..." Phineas hesitated for a moment before saying, "I think you should all leave me alone so I can check my vessel for damages!"

Jedidiah and Matthew were both taken aback by his uncharacteristic attitude. Neither of them had ever seen him act this way before, however, they didn't want to question him about it in front of Myra. "Alright, Phineas. We'll leave you to it," Jedidiah said, exchanging a knowing glance with Matthew. They nodded in agreement and rejoined the others.

****

Later that evening, the Davenport Ranch was abuzz with lively activity. The sprawling landscape of green pastures and rolling hills, bathed in the golden hue of the setting sun, provided a majestic backdrop. Jedidiah's Victorian-style home, adorned with softly glowing lanterns, stood proudly at the center. The well-tended gardens burst with late-summer blooms, their scents mingling with the aroma of roasted meats and freshly baked bread, courtesy of Pat Bennington.

People from all over the valley mingled, sharing stories and enjoying the festive atmosphere. A local band played lively tunes from a makeshift stage, their melodies carrying on the breeze and blending with the sounds of laughter and chatter. Matthew Colton entertained a group of children with animated tales of their past adventures, his eyes widening dramatically as he said, "And then, we narrowly escaped the gunfire by hiding in the clouds. They never saw where we went!"

Meanwhile, Phineas B. Hargroves captivated curious townsfolk with his latest invention. Holding up a small, intricate device, he explained, "This here is a prototype for an automatic milking machine. It will revolutionize dairy farming, mark my words."

Pat Bennington ensured everyone had their fill, bustling around the large outdoor kitchen area and calling out, "Don't be shy now, there's plenty for everyone!" Nearby, a spirited game of horseshoes drew cheers and jeers, as participants good-naturedly competed. "Close, but not close enough!"

The ranch was alive with the
sounds of laughter and music.

one man laughed as his friend narrowly missed the stake. Couples danced under the soft glow of lanterns, twirling and swaying in sync with the lively beat of the music, their laughter ringing out into the evening.

As the festivities continued, Myra Wilhelmina Bancroft landed her airship, the Enigma, in the large open space separating the two hangars. The arrival of the majestic vessel drew many admiring glances. The sleek design of the Enigma, with its polished brass and intricate detailing, was most impressive.

As promised, one of Jedidiah's hired hands was waiting for her with a horse and buggy to carry her to the main house. The ride was brief, but Myra took in the serene beauty of the ranch, appreciating the well-tended fields and the distant silhouettes of grazing horses.

Jedidiah made his way through the crowd, greeting guests and ensuring everyone was having a good time. He spotted Myra climbing out of the carriage and approached her with a welcoming smile. "I hope you're enjoying the evening, Myra," Jedidiah said, as he offered her a glass of lemonade.

"This place is amazing," Myra remarked, her eyes sparkling with admiration. "Your ranch is quite impressive. How many acres do you own?"

"Thank you," he smiled and modestly replied,

"Slightly over ten thousand."

Myra's eyes widened as she didn't expect such a large number. The Davenport Ranch was more grand than she realized.

Wanting to change the subject, Jedidiah glanced around at the various people and said, "I suppose you've already gotten a chance to meet everyone here."

"I think so," Myra replied, then suddenly noticed an older woman approaching them with a stern look on her face. It was Davenport's housekeeper, Agatha Porter. "Wait, I don't think I've met her," she added, motioning towards the newcomer.

"Jed!" Agatha's voice cut sharply through the conversation as she drew near, flailing her arms in exasperation. "That heated water contraption of yours has sprung a leak and is flooding the kitchen!"

Jedidiah's ranch was known for its innovative amenities, many of which he had invented himself. Agatha was referring to Jedidiah's heated water system that provided warm baths and comfortable living conditions even in the cooler months. He had placed a storage tank in the tower attached to the side of his house and installed a fire pit under it to heat the water. This storage unit was filled by another tank at a higher elevation, providing a flow of both hot and cold running water to the entire house.

"It's probably just a gasket," the young inventor replied calmly. He turned and excused himself from the adventurous airship captain to take care of the issue.

After Jedidiah had gone, Agatha's demeanor lightened, and she introduced herself to Myra. "I'm Jed's housekeeper," she said. "You must be that woman airship captain I've been hearing about!"

Myra couldn't help but chuckle at the directness of the other woman. "Last I checked, yes," she replied.

As they continued their conversation, Matthew Colton and Tom Miller were not far away, engaging in a discussion of their own.

Tom had approached Matthew a moment prior with a frustrated expression. "Matt, I don't think it's fair that you're bringing in Lucas Benson from Sheffield to run the Spoon Fork office while you're away," he said, clearly disappointed.

Ever since Matthew had taken over the main branch of the Davenport Dispatch & Delivery Company, Tom Miller had been working as his personal assistant.

"It's out of my hands, Tom," Matthew replied. "Jed said he would feel more comfortable leaving someone in charge with a little more experience." He paused, trying to find a way not to hurt the younger man's feelings, but couldn't think of one.

So he just said, "And I agree with him."

"Experience?" Tom suddenly looked even more dejected. "If this is because of my age, you know I turn eighteen next week. I'm the same age that Mr. Davenport was when he took over the company."

Matthew Colton sighed and shook his head. "Look, I understand how you feel, but like I said, it's out of my hands. If you want to try and talk to Jed, go right ahead. Maybe you can convince him to change his mind."

"You wouldn't mind me going over your head?" the younger man asked hesitantly.

Matthew laughed. "I told you it wasn't my decision, so you wouldn't be going over my head."

Tom's face suddenly brightened, and he thanked Matt before turning on his heel and walking away to look for the owner of the freight company.

Meanwhile, the same shadowy figure who had been eavesdropping earlier arrived at the party. He slipped quietly through the crowd, listening to more conversations. When he spotted Myra Wilhelmina Bancroft talking to Agatha Porter, his eyes widened in panic. He spun around to leave but collided with Tom Miller, knocking him flat on his back.

"Watch it, kid!" the mysterious stranger shouted as he pushed his way through the crowd and disappeared.

"Kid?" Tom huffed as he stood up. "I bet that

dolt isn't any older than I am." After dusting himself off, he continued his search for Davenport. A fellow party guest mentioned seeing Jedidiah go inside the house a few minutes earlier.

Stepping up onto the porch, Tom nervously reached for the doorknob. He hesitated briefly before turning it and calling out, "Mr. Davenport... I mean Jed..."

"I'm in here!" Jedidiah's voice echoed from the kitchen.

Tom stepped into the room to find his employer standing on the counter, tightening a fitting on the pipe coming from the ceiling. "Is this a bad time?" Tom asked, shifting his weight anxiously.

"Not at all!" the young inventor replied as he turned the valve next to the basin and steaming hot water began to come out. "I just finished. What do you need, Tom? You enjoying the party?"

"Yes sir," the younger man replied. "This is the best shindig I've ever been to. It's the perfect end to Founder's Day."

Jedidiah jumped down from the counter and looked at his employee. He could tell there was something else on his mind. The way he stood and the expression on his face told Davenport exactly what he was thinking. Before young Miller could say anything else, Jedidiah decided to speak.

"You know, Tom," he began, "I really appreciate how hard you've been working the past few months. Matt has been telling me some really good things about you. He said if we give you a few more months, you'll be ready to run that office all by yourself."

"He did?" the younger man suddenly brightened up.

"I know you've learned a lot already, and you'll have the chance to learn a lot more from Lucas Benson. I think by the next time Matt and I go on another adventure, you'll be more than ready."

"No fooling?" Tom asked excitedly.

Jedidiah smiled, nodded, and replied, "No fooling!"

The younger man suddenly seemed much more satisfied with the decision to leave someone else in charge. He thanked Jedidiah and turned on his heel to rejoin the party.

****

Later in the evening, Jedidiah noticed Myra standing alone by the porch, gazing up at the stars. He approached her, sensing an opportunity to learn more about the enigmatic woman.

"You know," he began, "I've always been fascinated by your experiences. Could you tell me more about how you got started with airships and your first real adventure?"

Myra smiled, taking a sip of her lemonade. "I

was quite up in years when I had my first introduction to the world of air travel. It wasn't until the age of thirty-three that I traveled to Paris to witness Henri Giffard's first steam-powered airship. I'll never forget the first time I saw that marvel of the sky." Myra's eyes lit up as she began to recall the event.

****

It was 1852, and Paris was alive with innovation and excitement. The city was a beacon of progress, and I was there, eager to witness history in the making. Henri Giffard's airship was a marvel—an enormous cigar-shaped balloon powered by a small steam engine. It was only three horsepower and sailed along at a moderate six miles per hour, but it was the most beautiful thing I had ever seen.

I remember standing among the crowd of onlookers, my eyes wide with wonder. The airship, this massive dirigible, loomed above us, casting a shadow over the city. The sight was breathtaking, unlike anything I had ever seen.

I was there with my sister Rebecca. She hadn't come for the same reason I had. Her main interest was just in visiting Paris. However, after she saw the airship, she too was taken in by its majestic grandeur.

'Rebecca,' I said, nudging her, 'this is going to change everything. Can you imagine soaring through the skies?'

Rebecca nodded, barely able to contain her excitement. 'It's like something out of a dream,' she said.

My heart raced as I watched Giffard's airship ascend and glide effortlessly through the sky. The crowd erupted in cheers, and I felt this surge of excitement. That moment, seeing that airship take flight, ignited a passion in me. I knew I had to be a part of this new frontier.

I returned to London and began studying engineering and aeronautics. Naturally, I faced many challenges as a woman in a male-dominated field, but my determination never wavered.

Shortly after I turned thirty-five, I joined an expedition to explore uncharted territories in Africa. It was my first major adventure, and it tested every bit of knowledge and courage I had.

We traveled mostly on foot but also by steamboat. We faced severe storms and mechanical failures aboard the boat," Myra said, a hint of pride in her voice. "But we persevered. That journey taught me resilience and the importance of never giving up.

****

"The lure of adventure and, of course, my fascination with airships only deepened after that," Myra concluded.

"Myra," Jedidiah said softly, "you've led an incredible life. No wonder you're such a skilled captain."

The older woman smiled and said, "Every challenge, every setback, it all shaped who I am, and there's still so much for me to learn."

"And what exactly have you learned?" A loud voice suddenly boomed from a few feet away. "How to sell books and dime-store novels based on your exaggerated adventures?"

Jedidiah and Myra both turned to see Phineas B. Hargroves standing before them.

"Phineas!" Jedidiah called his friend's name. "What's the matter with you? Why are you being so rude to Ms. Bancroft? She's a guest here at the Davenport ranch!"

"Are you still upset that I hurt your pride by rescuing you earlier?" the older woman scoffed. "If that's the case, I'd be glad to hang you from the side of your ship again and let you drift away into the clouds!"

"Don't you think you've done enough to me today?" Phineas shouted, taking a step back. His eyes flashed with anger but also a hint of hurt that he quickly tried to mask.

"What have I done besides save your life?"

Myra demanded, squaring off with him. She felt her heart rate increase, not just from the argument but from the residual adrenaline of the rescue.

"I recognized the man who attacked me!" Phineas jabbed a finger in Myra's direction, his voice trembling with indignation.

Myra's eyes narrowed. "What does that mean?" She glanced at Jedidiah for support but found him watching silently, his expression unreadable.

"You know what it means!" Phineas's voice dropped to a low growl, his fists clenching at his sides. He felt a bead of sweat trickle down his temple and wiped it away with an irritated swipe. Without saying a word, he turned and stormed off.

As the older man was leaving, Jedidiah turned to Myra and asked, "Why do I feel like there's something more going on between the two of you than just what happened today?"

The adventurous woman took a deep breath before responding, "You can say that again. It all started..."

Before Myra could even begin to explain, her words were cut short by a deafening blast that shattered the calm evening.

Suddenly, the ground shook beneath them as a shockwave of heat and noise roared through the air. Screams erupted from all directions, and a chorus of panic filled the night. Jedidiah's heart pounded in his chest. He quickly scanned the area, trying to comprehend what had just happened.

Through the chaos, one of Jedidiah's hired hands came stumbling forward, his face pale and eyes wide with fear. "There's been an explosion!" he gasped, struggling to catch his breath.

CHAPTER IV

Barnyard Blazes

"Explosion!" Jedidiah exclaimed, echoing the words of the panic-stricken man. "Where?"

"The barn!" he gasped, pointing frantically. "There's smoke and flames coming from the hay next to it!"

Jedidiah's heart sank as he remembered the crates of fireworks stored inside for the evening's grand finale, along with several boxes of dynamite used for clearing stumps. If the fire reached them, the results would be catastrophic. The realization hit Davenport like a punch to the gut, the joy of the evening evaporating in an instant.

"Everyone, to the barn!" Jedidiah shouted, spurring the crowd into action. "We need to contain the fire before it reaches the explosives!"

The crowd quickly responded, gathering buckets of water and sand. Jim Davis and Matthew Colton led the charge, organizing a bucket brigade.

The heat was intense, and the crackling of flames filled the air. Jedidiah, coughing from the smoke, spotted the source of the explosion—an open crate of dynamite. One of the sticks was missing.

"We need to get all of these explosives out of here!" he yelled, watching as the fire crept further inside the building.

Suddenly, Phineas B. Hargroves arrived, his face set with determination. "Jed, use this!" he shouted, handing over a strange-looking contraption.

"What is it?" the frustrated ranch owner asked in confusion.

"It's a portable fire extinguisher," the eccentric older man explained. "I've designed it myself. Now, put it on!"

The device was a marvel of ingenuity. Constructed from brass and copper, it featured a cylindrical tank mounted on a sturdy leather harness that could be worn on the back. Attached to the tank was a coiled hose made of reinforced rubber, ending in a brass nozzle with various levers and dials. The tank was adorned with gears and pressure gauges, giving it an intricate, almost whimsical appearance.

Jedidiah strapped on the harness and felt the weight of the contraption. He lowered his goggles and adjusted the dials as Phineas instructed, then

Jedidiah strapped on the harness and
felt the weight of the contraption. He
lowered his goggles and adjusted the dials.

pulled the lever. A powerful stream of chemical foam shot out of the nozzle, hissing as it smothered the flames.

"This is incredible!" Jedidiah shouted over the roar of the fire. The foam spread quickly, creating a thick, fire-retardant barrier that suffocated the flames. Slowly but surely, the fire began to recede.

As the flames were brought under control and the last crate of fireworks was safely removed, the crowd breathed a collective sigh of relief. Exhausted but grateful, Jedidiah surveyed the charred but still-standing barn. The explosion had left a gaping hole in one side, with smoke still drifting out in thin wisps. The wooden beams inside were splintered, and blackened patches marked where the fire had taken hold. Despite the damage, Jedidiah was thankful for everyone's swift actions in containing the blaze.

"That was too close," Jim Davis said, wiping sweat from his brow. "What happened? Who did this?"

Jedidiah glanced at the open crate of dynamite. "I'm not sure," he admitted. "But we need to find out. It could have been much worse."

The foreman stepped forward, his expression serious. "If someone is targeting you, we all need to be on guard."

"Targeting Jed?" Agatha Porter coughed, trying to clear smoke from her lungs. "Why would anyone want to harm Jed?"

"Yeah, all that nasty business with the railroad is long over!" Pat Bennington spoke up. "If anyone's got a target on their backs, it's probably Phineas or that Bancroft lady. They're the ones everyone's betting on in the upcoming race."

"But then shouldn't the explosion have been closer to the hangars where the airships are?" Jim Davis countered.

"Anyone of us could have been the target," Myra interjected defensively. "Phineas, Jedidiah, or myself. We're all three entered in the race."

There was a collective gasp from those nearby, as they realized for the first time that Jedidiah was competing in the sky race.

"Myra Wilhelmina Bancroft!" Phineas B. Hargroves suddenly exclaimed.

"What?" Myra asked, clearly puzzled.

"You've never learned to keep your mouth shut, have you?"

"Land o' Goshen!" Pat Bennington exclaimed. "Jed, are you really gonna be in the race?"

"They didn't know?" Myra looked genuinely surprised.

"We do now!" Agatha Porter interjected with disdain. "Why didn't you tell us, Jed?"

"I only told Matthew, the professor, and Sheriff Thompson. I didn't even tell the sheriff until earlier today," Jedidiah replied, slightly annoyed. He turned to Myra, the source of his unintentionally revealed secret, and asked, "How did you find out I was entered?"

"Yeah," Matthew Colton chimed in. "Jed paid extra to keep his name off the registry until the day before the race."

"I'm friends with one of the board members," Myra explained casually. "I was visiting them when I happened to glance at the full list of contestants. It said, clear as day, 'Jedidiah Davenport and his Airship,' but I didn't realize it wasn't public knowledge."

"Well, it doesn't matter now," Jedidiah remarked. "The cat's out of the bag." His resolve hardening, he added, "Let's just find out who did this and stop them!"

"Mr. Davenport..." Jedidiah suddenly felt a tug on his pant leg. He turned around and saw a small child staring up at him.

"Go ahead, Billy," a plump matronly woman standing behind him said, giving him a little push forward. "Tell him!"

"Tell me?" Jedidiah asked, confused. "Tell me what, Billy? Did you see who did this?"

"Kind of, Mr. Davenport..."

Jedidiah crouched down to be at eye level with him. "What did you see?" he asked gently.

The small boy hesitated, glancing back at his mother for reassurance before speaking. "I was playing near the barn when... I saw a man go inside. He was carrying a stick that looked like one of those big firecrackers..."

"Billy!" the matronly woman interjected. "Tell him what really happened!"

"Yes, ma..." Billy reluctantly began again, "Mr. Davenport, I didn't know it was dynamite. I thought it was a firecracker, honest!"

"Billy, did you light that explosive and toss it behind that big round bale of hay near the barn?"

"I guess I sort of did..."

Suddenly everyone around breathed a collective sigh of relief and started laughing. None laughed harder than Pat Bennington, who said, "Take it easy on him, Jed. He may have the face of a hardened criminal, but I think he can be reformed."

The boy, who couldn't have been over eight years old, looked confused as all the adults, including his mother, burst into laughter.

"You're right, Pat," the ranch owner agreed. "I think he's learned his lesson." He looked directly at the child and said, "Next time, just leave the fireworks to the adults."

After the laughter died down and everyone began to return to the party, Billy tugged on Jedidiah's pant leg once again. "Mr. Davenport, there's more. After the explosion, I really did see a man running away while everyone was helping to put out the fire." The boy pulled out a small, crumpled piece of paper from his pocket. "He dropped this."

Jedidiah took the paper and unfolded it carefully. It was a torn piece of a larger document, bearing part of a logo he didn't recognize and handwritten numbers that resembled a code or a note.

"Good job, Billy. This might be important," Jedidiah said, patting the boy on the head. "Thank you for telling me."

Phineas glanced over his shoulder and said, "That logo seems vaguely familiar, but I can't place it."

Myra, who had been quietly observing, stepped forward. "Looks familiar to me too."

"It's probably nothing," Jedidiah remarked as he folded the paper and placed it in his pocket. "But I'll hang on to it just in case."

Just as the band began to play again, Sheriff Thompson and his two deputies rode up. As they dismounted, the sheriff told his men to enjoy the party. Then, he turned to Jedidiah and the others, informing them that they never found the man who had assaulted Phineas earlier.

"No sign of him anywhere?" Jedidiah asked curiously.

"We followed him and his partner up into the hills before we lost their trail," Sheriff Thompson explained. "We did, however, spot the men from the railroad working on the tracks. They've made some impressive progress. I'd say they've covered nearly one hundred and fifty miles in the past three months."

"At this rate, they'll reach Spoon Fork even sooner than we expected," Jedidiah remarked with a pleased tone.

"Wait a minute, Sheriff," Myra Wilhelmina Bancroft suddenly spoke up, "Did you say him *and* his partner? There was only one man up there with Phineas when I rescued him."

"We found two sets of tracks leading away from the airship," he explained. "It only makes sense, considering the glass from the window was on the inside."

"Gosh! That means somebody broke it from the outside!" Matthew Colton excitedly stated, realizing the obvious fact that everyone else had already grasped.

"I wonder who it could have been," Myra pondered, puzzled.

"As if you didn't know!" Phineas shouted.

"What is that supposed to mean?" the adventurous airship captain demanded, stepping toward her accuser. "Are you trying to imply that I sent those men to attack you?"

"I'm not saying anything, but that does seem logical, don't you think?" Phineas tried to calm himself by taking a deep breath. "After all, the man who hung me out to dry was the same one who attacked me in my hotel room earlier this year!"

Jedidiah suddenly realized that his friend and mentor was right. As he reflected on the attack he had witnessed through his telescopic lenses, it dawned on him. The man involved was the same one he had seen running into the hallway the night he and Phineas had met in Wichita.

"Now hold on, Hargroves," Sheriff Thompson spoke up. "That's a serious accusation. Do you have any proof?"

"Only years of intuition!" Phineas replied, his tone defiant.

Myra took a deep breath, trying to steady her voice. "If I had hired them to attack you, why would I have risked my own life to save you?" She searched Phineas's face, looking for any sign of understanding.

"Attention, maybe?" Phineas shrugged his shoulders. "Try to make yourself seem innocent when you're really a notorious villain." He turned away, running a hand through his disheveled hair, trying to regain some semblance of composure.

"Notorious..." Myra's hands balled into fists. She felt the familiar pang of frustration when dealing with stubborn individuals. "If I wanted attention, I wouldn't need to risk my neck for it." Taking a deep breath, she stopped herself before saying something she would regret. Myra turned to

Jedidiah and said, "I'm sorry my presence here has caused such an inconvenience to your party. I think it would be in my best interest and everyone else's if I were to leave."

"Wait, don't leave angry," Jedidiah tried to stop the older woman from storming away. "I'm sure there's a perfectly good explanation for all of this."

"Besides, Ms. Bancroft," Matthew spoke up, "it's almost time for us to set off the fireworks. You don't want to miss that!"

Myra turned back and looked at everyone, even Phineas B. Hargroves. The eccentric inventor merely said, "By all means, don't leave on my behalf. You've already lit the fire, might as well stay for the explosion."

"Poor choice of words, Hargy..." Pat Bennington suddenly howled with laughter as he motioned towards the scorched barn with the giant hole in the side. "Poor choice of words!"

Choosing to ignore the rotund man's comments, everyone looked to the adventurous airship captain for a response. Myra sighed as she reluctantly agreed to stay. "Very well, but the moment the fireworks are done, so am I!"

After the remaining people separated and rejoined the party, Jedidiah, Matthew, and Jim Davis picked up the crates of fireworks and made their way to the area where they had planned to set them off. Despite all the chaos, there was still a sense of anticipation in the air.

"Every time we think we have things under control, something else blows up in our faces," Matthew muttered, glancing back at the barn.

Jedidiah nodded, a grim look on his face. "It's like we're just putting out one fire after another. Both metaphorically and literally."

Matthew smirked. "And we always seem to be one step behind. It's exhausting."

"Yeah," Jedidiah agreed. "But we don't have the luxury of giving up. Too much rides on us staying ahead of the chaos." Jedidiah glanced over in the direction of the small boy and his mother and said, "At least this time it really was just an accident."

After setting all the fireworks in place, Jedidiah announced, "Alright, everyone, it's time!"

The crowd gathered in the field, looking up at the sky in eager anticipation. Jedidiah gave the signal, and the first firework shot into the air, exploding in a brilliant display of colors. Cheers and applause erupted from the crowd as more fireworks followed, each one more spectacular than the last.

Jedidiah stood back, watching the joy on everyone's faces. For a moment, the troubles and tensions were forgotten, replaced by the simple pleasure of the celebration. Despite the setbacks, the party had been a success.

Meanwhile, Tom Miller, who had been getting

himself a glass of punch, suddenly noticed a shadowy figure maneuvering its way through the crowd. Even in the dark, Tom could see them sneaking into the stables. Moments later, they reemerged on horseback and headed towards the field where the hangars and airships were.

Tom turned on his heel and started to go tell someone but decided this might be his chance to show how valuable he was. With great determination, the young man rushed over to his own horse, mounted it, and headed off in pursuit.

Tom urged his horse to a gallop, following the shadowy figure through the darkness. The mysterious stranger seemed to be riding with a clear purpose. Tom kept a safe distance, careful not to alert the rider to his presence.

As they approached the hangars, Tom slowed his horse and dismounted, deciding to proceed on foot to avoid detection. He crept closer, hiding behind a stack of crates as he watched the figure tie their horse and slip inside the newly constructed building.

Tom's heart raced as he tried to decide what to do next. He knew he needed to find out who this person was and what they were up to, but he also didn't want to confront them alone. Taking a deep breath, he decided to quietly slip inside, keeping to the shadows.

Inside the hangar, the mysterious stranger

moved quickly, heading towards Phineas B. Hargroves' prized airship, the Icarus. The figure appeared to be tampering with the ship, and Tom could see the glint of metal tools in the dim light.

Realizing the urgency of the situation, Tom quickly debated going for help or taking this person on himself. Ultimately, he decided to take matters into his own hands.

"Stop right there!" the young man shouted, stepping out of the shadows.

The mysterious stranger froze and slowly turned towards him, but Tom didn't give him much time to react. He leaped forward in a flying tackle. "Got you!" Tom grunted, pinning him to the ground.

"Get off of me!" the stranger shouted. He was about the same size as Tom and struggled to push him away.

"No!" Tom screamed. "You're coming with me!"

"Look, kid," he shouted, "I'm not going anywhere with you!"

"Kid!" Tom was immediately insulted. He stopped wrestling with the saboteur and looked directly into his face. Even in the dim light, he recognized the man as the same one who had bumped into him and knocked him down earlier. "Who are you?"

"Puddin' Tane!" the unknown stranger shouted. Taking advantage of Tom's sudden surprise, he was able to shove him off and spring to his feet. "Now back up, kid. I don't want to hurt you!"

Instantly furious from being called a kid once again, Tom took a step forward. "Why do you keep calling me that? You can't be any older than I am!"

"Just stay back!" the would-be saboteur shouted. "I'm warning you!"

"I don't take orders from no-name riffraff!" Tom took another step forward.

With wild, frightened eyes, the stranger shouted, "No! Don't!!!"

Tom took one more step forward, but just as he was about to make his move, he was struck from behind!

CHAPTER V

Hidden Dangers

Tom Miller's head throbbed as he regained consciousness, the dim light of the hangar casting eerie shadows on the walls. He blinked, clearing the fog from his mind, and realized he was lying on the cold, hard floor. The distant sounds of the festival were muffled by the thick walls.

Groaning, Tom pushed himself up to a seated position, his hand instinctively going to the back of his head where a lump was forming. He winced at the touch, the pain sharp and immediate.

"*What happened?*" he muttered to himself, trying to piece together the events that had led him there.

He remembered following the shadowy figure, the confrontation, and then… darkness. Someone had hit him from behind. Tom's eyes darted around the hangar, searching for any sign of the saboteur. The Icarus loomed large in the center of the space, its sleek lines and intricate design a testament to Phineas B. Hargroves' genius.

A sense of urgency gripped Tom. He needed to alert Jedidiah and the others about what he had seen. Struggling to his feet, he staggered toward the hangar doors, his steps unsteady but determined. As he pushed the heavy doors open, the cool night air hit his face, refreshing and invigorating.

Tom scanned the area outside the hangar, hoping to spot the stranger, but there was no sign of him. The festival was still in full swing, oblivious to the danger he had just been through. He needed to find Jedidiah.

Before Tom could take more than a few steps, he was suddenly attacked from behind again. This time, a burlap bag was draped over his head, preventing him from seeing. Immediately after, he felt a rope being wrapped around him, pinning his arms to his side. The young man was helpless as his feet were forcefully pulled out from under him.

Back at the party, the final burst of fireworks lit up the night sky, casting a kaleidoscope of colors over the Davenport Ranch. The guests applauded and cheered, their faces aglow with excitement. Jedidiah watched with a sense of pride and satisfaction, happy that the day's events had brought so much joy to everyone.

As the last sparkles faded into the night, the band played a gentle tune, signaling the end of the celebration. Guests began to gather their belongings and say their goodbyes, expressing their gratitude for Davenport's hospitality.

"Thanks, Jed, for a wonderful evening," Sheriff Thompson said, shaking his hand. "It's exactly what this town needed."

"Glad you enjoyed it," Jedidiah replied, smiling warmly. "It's always a pleasure to bring everyone together."

Phineas B. Hargroves approached his earlier irritation seemingly forgotten. "Well, my dear boy, it appears your party was a grand success," he said, clapping Jedidiah on the shoulder. "But I must say, I'm looking forward to getting back to work on the Icarus. The race will be here before you know it!"

"Thanks, Phineas," Jedidiah replied, noting the inventor's restored spirits. "Are you starting on it tonight?"

The eccentric older man merely laughed and said, "I'm anxious, not obsessive. I'll begin first thing in the morning!"

"Good idea," Jedidiah agreed. "We should all get some rest because tomorrow will be a busy day."

As the last of the guests departed, Myra Wilhelmina Bancroft lingered a moment before returning to her airship. She approached Jedidiah, her expression thoughtful.

"I appreciate the invitation, Jed," Myra said.

"Despite the excitement and you-know-who, it was a pleasant evening."

"I'm glad you stayed," Jedidiah replied sincerely. "And I look forward to a friendly competition when we meet again in a couple of weeks."

Myra smiled a hint of mischief in her eyes. "Friendly, yes, but just remember it is a competition and I won't be holding back. Therefore, I don't expect you to either."

With that, she made a gesturing motion of tipping an invisible hat and made her way to the buggy that was waiting to return her to the Enigma. Jedidiah watched her go, a sense of anticipation for the adventures ahead stirring within him.

As the night settled and the ranch grew quiet, Jedidiah made his way back inside. He couldn't shake the feeling that something was wrong, but he brushed it aside, attributing it to the excitement and chaos of the festival. Unbeknownst to him, Tom Miller's fate was hanging in the balance.

The ranch slowly descended into a peaceful silence. The last of the guests had departed, their laughter and conversations now a distant memory. The night air was cool and still, settling over the ranch like a blanket. Stars twinkled above, casting a gentle glow on the quiet landscape. The soft rustling of leaves and the occasional call of a night bird were the only sounds breaking the silence.

Inside the hangar, Tom's absence went unnoticed, his struggle a secret held by the shadows of the night.

****

The next morning, Phineas B. Hargroves was up at the crack of dawn, his mind already buzzing with plans for tweaks to his famed aircraft. As he descended the stairs of Jedidiah's Victorian home, he was immediately enticed by the smell of breakfast cooking. The aroma of fresh coffee, sizzling bacon, and buttery biscuits filled the air, promising a hearty start to the day.

Phineas entered the kitchen to find Pat Bennington bustling about, humming a cheerful tune as he flipped pancakes. "Morning, Hargy," Pat greeted him with a grin. "Hope you're ready for a big breakfast. I'm sure you've got a lot to do today."

"Hargroves," Phineas corrected, taking a seat at the table. "Nevertheless, good morning, Pat." The eccentric older man reached over, picked up a folded cloth napkin, and said, "Indeed, the race preparations are never-ending. But first, I need fuel for energy. Your cooking should do the trick."

As Phineas poured himself a cup of coffee, Jedidiah entered the kitchen, looking refreshed but contemplative.

"Morning, Phineas. Morning, Pat," he said,

nodding to each. He looked around the room and noticed Matthew Colton hadn't come down yet. "You mean I actually beat Matt to breakfast for once?"

"Not by much," Agatha Porter remarked as she entered the room. "I heard him upstairs washing up. He'll be down soon." As she said this, she took her place at the table.

When the older woman first became employed at the Davenport Ranch, she took all of her meals in her room, but as time went by she began to feel more comfortable. Jedidiah eventually convinced her to start sitting at the table and eating with everyone else.

Phineas took a sip of his coffee, savoring the rich flavor. "Well, Jed, it looks like today is going to be another busy one. We need to ensure everything is in tip-top shape for the race. After I make some adjustments to the Icarus, would you like me to look over the Phoenix?"

Jedidiah smiled mysteriously and said, "Thanks, but I don't think that will be necessary."

"My dear boy," the eccentric older man replied, "You do realize the race is in two weeks, don't you? You do wish to do everything you can to win, don't you?"

Jedidiah nodded. "I'll definitely be giving it my all." He smiled as he said, "But two weeks is plenty of time. Remember we built the Phoenix in not much more time than that."

"I just feel like you're not taking this seriously enough."

"Don't worry," Jedidiah assured his friend. "I'll be giving you and everyone else in the race a run for their money!"

Just as he said this, Matthew Colton came bounding down the stairs and into the kitchen. "Morning, everybody," he greeted them as he took a seat. "What's on the agenda for today?"

"I plan to perform some modifications on the Icarus," Phineas said, setting his coffee cup down. "There are a few adjustments I want to make to the steam engine to ensure it performs at its best." He glanced over at Jedidiah with distaste. "I've offered to look over the Phoenix as well, but I guess some people are afraid I'll tune it down instead of up, to give myself an edge in the race!"

Jedidiah laughed and shook his head, "I didn't say that. I just said that it wasn't necessary. Look, Phineas, if it will make you feel better, go right ahead. After you've finished with your ship, you have my permission to tune up the Phoenix as much as you want!"

"What do you have for me to do today?" Matthew Colton asked curiously. "It's Sunday, and the freight office is closed, so I know you'll have something for me to do around here."

Jedidiah nodded. "We need to go over the race

route again, make sure we have all the necessary supplies, and check the weather reports for the next few weeks. We can't afford any surprises."

Phineas huffed, "Well, at least you're taking some part of this race seriously."

As the morning sun climbed higher in the sky, the group finished their breakfast and prepared to tackle the day's work. The twin hangars housing the two famed airships were now bathed in the rays of the sun. Inside, the temperatures were already starting to rise. Tom Miller, who had been struggling against his restraints all night, finally passed out from exhaustion just moments before Phineas B. Hargroves entered the building to start work.

Phineas climbed aboard the Icarus, completely unaware of the bound individual hidden under the boarding ramp. His mind focused on the modifications he had planned for the steam engine. The hum of activity inside the hangar was soon accompanied by the clinking of tools and the occasional muttered exclamation as Phineas immersed himself in his work.

Meanwhile, Jedidiah and Matthew had settled into the study, a space filled with maps, charts, and various navigational instruments. They spread the race route out on the large table and began reviewing the checkpoints and potential hazards they might encounter along the way.

Phineas B. Hargroves prepared to work
on the Icarus, unaware of Tom Miller
lying bound only a few feet from him.

"We need to ensure we have all the necessary supplies," Jedidiah said, tracing the route with his finger. "And we should double-check the weather reports for each segment of the race."

Matthew nodded in agreement. "I'll make a list of everything we need and start gathering the supplies. We can't afford any delays once the race begins."

As they worked, the morning's calm contrasted sharply with the urgency of their preparations. The ranch, still quiet from the previous night's festivities, began to stir with the sounds of activity as the day progressed.

Back in the hangar, Phineas finished his initial checks on the Icarus and decided to take a short break before tackling the more intricate modifications. He wiped his hands and glanced around the hangar. Stepping outside, he looked at the other building, recalling his conversation with Jedidiah.

"Well, I suppose a quick inspection wouldn't hurt," Phineas muttered to himself as he walked over and went inside. He went straight to the Phoenix and climbed aboard. Phineas glanced over the various systems, making mental notes of any adjustments that might be needed.

After spending only a few minutes with Jedidiah's ship, Phineas turned and headed back to work on his own vessel. Outside, the ranch continued its usual rhythm.

Around noon, Jedidiah and Matthew finished their planning and decided to check on Phineas. They arrived to find him adjusting the steam engine, which was huffing and puffing away at only half-strength.

"How's everything going?" Jedidiah asked the older man as they approached him.

"My dear boy," Phineas replied with a look of concern on his face. "I don't know what's wrong with my engine. It's not maintaining pressure, and I keep hearing a blasted knocking sound coming from somewhere!"

"I hear it too!" Matthew exclaimed. "I think it's coming from below us!"

"That's the way it sounds!" Phineas replied. "But that's impossible. The only thing beneath us is the cargo hold, and I've already been down there. There's absolutely nothing that could be making that noise."

Jedidiah stood in thought, trying to puzzle out what it could be. "How about..." His sentence was cut short as a pipe sprung a huge leak, steam spewing and causing the engine to lose pressure and shut down.

The moment the steam finally stopped pouring out, Phineas rushed over to examine the damage. "Someone has been tampering with my ship. These pipes were punctured and temporarily sealed!"

"Gosh!" Matthew exclaimed. "It's a good thing they didn't burst while you were in mid-flight!"

"This is why I check things over thoroughly and constantly!" the older man shouted. "Someone must have snuck in here last night during the party and..." His thought was interrupted by the knocking sound coming from below them again. "What is that infernal racket?"

Before anyone could respond, faint hoarse cries for help began to lilt through the air.

With a look of determination, Phineas followed the sound outside the ship. Glancing under the ramp, he spotted a bound figure kicking the side of the airship with both feet in an attempt to get their attention. "Jed! Mat! Come quick!"

Within moments, Jedidiah and Matthew came running, their expressions turning to alarm as they spotted the prone figure. They quickly untied him and removed the burlap sack. They both gasped as they realized it was their friend Tom Miller. They wasted no time in picking him up and carrying him aboard the Icarus where they placed him on the bed in Phineas' cabin.

"Tom, can you hear me?" Jedidiah asked gently.

Tom stirred, groaning softly as he slowly regained consciousness. "Jed... I... I tried to warn you..." he mumbled, his voice weak.

"Warn us about what, Tom?" Matthew asked urgently. "What happened?"

Tom struggled to sit up, his eyes darting around as he tried to gather his thoughts. "There was someone... a saboteur... I followed him here... but he got the drop on me..."

"I knew it!" Phineas exclaimed. "Someone did tamper with my ship!"

Less concerned about the Icarus and more about the young man, Jedidiah and Matthew exchanged worried glances. "We need to get Tom to the doctor," Jedidiah said firmly. "He looks like he has taken quite a beating."

"Agreed," Matthew said. "Let's transfer him to the Phoenix. We'll never get this vessel off the ground with all those leaks, let alone all the way to Spoon Fork."

Phineas reluctantly agreed that the Icarus wasn't flight-worthy at the moment. "I'll go to the house and use the telegraph to inform the doctor you're coming."

Jedidiah nodded, recalling his investment in the telegraph company and the installation of an advanced communication system in his home. "Send a wire to the sheriff as well. Let him know there's been trouble."

As Jedidiah and Matthew carefully transferred Tom to the Phoenix, Phineas hurried towards the house, determination set on his face. He reached the study and quickly made his way to the telegraph corner, where Jedidiah's ingenious invention stood ready.

The device was a marvel of modern engineering: a combination of a telegraph and a typewriter designed to streamline communication. It featured a sleek brass frame with polished wooden accents. The typewriter keyboard was flanked by two spools, one for recording and the other for playing back pre-recorded messages, similar to a player piano. This allowed for efficient sending and receiving of messages without the need for Morse code expertise.

Phineas sat down and rapidly typed out the message to Doc Stone, the keys clacking with urgency:

"DOC STONE, STOP. EMERGENCY STOP. TOM MILLER INJURED STOP. NEED MEDICAL ATTENTION IMMEDIATELY STOP. ARRIVING PHOENIX AIRSHIP SOON STOP. JEDIDIAH DAVENPORT STOP."

Phineas removed the newly recorded roll and transferred it to the other spool on the machine, which automatically converted it into a telegraph signal as the keys fell into the punched holes. The device hummed and clicked as it sent the message over the wire. As soon as the message was sent, Phineas prepared a second one for Sheriff Thompson:

"SHERIFF THOMPSON, STOP. SABOTAGE ATTEMPT CONFIRMED STOP. TOM MILLER ASSAULTED STOP. PHOENIX AIRSHIP EN ROUTE TO SPOON FORK WITH VICTIM STOP. REQUEST IMMEDIATE ASSISTANCE AT DOC STONE'S OFFICE STOP. JEDIDIAH DAVENPORT STOP."

The second message was swiftly transmitted, and Phineas watched as the typewriter began to print incoming acknowledgments from both recipients. The invention was truly remarkable, ensuring that communication was clear and immediate.

Satisfied that help was on the way, Phineas dashed back outside. The Phoenix was already ascending into the sky and sailing towards town.

"Hang in there, Tom," Jedidiah said as he expertly piloted the vessel. The Phoenix glided along smoothly, the landscape rolling by beneath them as they continued to gain altitude.

As they were approaching the streets of Spoon Fork, a sharp whistle split the air. Jedidiah's eyes widened in alarm as the pressure gauge started to drop. "Matthew, check the engine!" he shouted over the noise.

Matthew rushed to the engine room, his heart pounding. He examined the machinery, looking for the source of the problem. "Jed, we've got a leak!"

CHAPTER VI

The Phoenix in Peril

"The pressure's dropping fast!" Matthew Colton shouted in terror. "The pipes have all sprung leaks, just like they did on the Icarus!"

Jedidiah Davenport's eyes widened as he felt the Phoenix shudder. Without the steam engine's propulsion system, the airship would begin to drift aimlessly through the sky. "Can you fix it?" Jedidiah asked, his voice tight with urgency as he struggled to keep his ship steady.

"I'm trying!" Matthew's hands moved quickly, tightening bolts and adjusting valves, but the leaks persisted, hissing angrily. Twice he burned himself on the steam escaping from the cracks. "I don't know if I can hold it much longer!"

Jedidiah glanced toward the sleeper cabin, where Tom Miller lay unconscious. He knew he was going to have to set his ship down somewhere. "Keep at it, Matt! We've got to make it to Doc's office!" Trying to remain positive he said, "At least it's just propulsion system and not..."

Suddenly, a loud hissing sound filled the cabin. Jedidiah's heart sank as he glanced above his head and spotted a large flapping hole in the canvas.

"At least it's not what?" Matthew asked innocently.

"That!" Jedidiah shouted pointing towards the torn fabric. "The airbag has been tampered with. We need to land now!"

As Matthew worked on the engine, Jedidiah focused on keeping the Phoenix as stable as possible. The buildings of Spoon Fork began coming into view. The airship wobbled precariously, but Jedidiah's skilled piloting kept them on course. Just as they passed over the main street, the pressure gauge dropped dangerously low, and the Phoenix began to slow rapidly.

"Hold on!" Jedidiah shouted, bracing for impact as he aimed the vessel toward the open field where the festival had been held the day before. "I've got to land, but without propulsion and with the airbag leaking, it's gonna be rough!"

The Phoenix descended rapidly, the landscape below rushing up to meet them. Jedidiah's knuckles turned white as he gripped the controls. The wind whipped around them, howling through the open windows as the ground approached.

The initial contact was brutal. The Phoenix hit

The airship wobbled precariously, but Jedidiah's skilled piloting kept them on course.

the ground with a bone-jarring thud, the impact jostling everyone on board violently. The wooden undercarriage splintered and cracked, sending shards flying as the vessel skidded along the ground. The airship dug a deep furrow into the dirt, throwing up clouds of dust and debris.

Jedidiah fought to keep the Phoenix steady, his muscles straining against the control levers. "Hang on!" he yelled again, his voice barely audible over the sound of splintering wood.

The airship's momentum carried it forward, the hull shuddering under the stress. Inside, loose items flew through the air, crashing into walls and floors. Matthew clung to a nearby support, his eyes wide with fear.

Outside, townsfolk, already alerted by the noise, rushed out to help. Men, women, and even children ran towards the field, their faces etched with concern and urgency. Some carried ropes, others brought tools, ready to assist however they could.

As the Phoenix finally came to a halt, a tense silence followed the roar of the crash. For a moment, the only sound was the creaking of the airship's frame as it settled into the freshly gouged earth. Then, the crowd of onlookers swarmed the vessel, shouting instructions and offering hands to help.

Sheriff Thompson and his deputies were among the first to arrive. "Jed! What happened? Is everyone alright?" he yelled from the ground.

"No time to explain," Jedidiah leaned over the rail of the ship and shouted back to the sheriff. He and Matthew immediately raced inside the cabin to lift Tom from one of the two cots. They exchanged puzzled looks as the young man was nowhere to be seen.

"Tom!" Jedidiah shouted. "Where are you?"

A hand suddenly popped up from between one of the cots and the wall of the cabin. The young man had been thrown there during the crash landing. "I'm down here!" Tom replied, pushing down on the cot to lift himself up. He actually appeared to be in better shape now than when they found him earlier.

"What'd I miss?" Tom asked innocently.

"Never mind," Matthew laughed. "Just be glad you missed it!"

"Just quite possibly the destruction of my airship" Jedidiah groaned. "That's all."

"Say, you look a lot better, Tom," Matthew remarked.

"Yeah, guess that little catnap I had was all I needed." Tom reached up and felt the back of his head, wincing as it was still throbbing.

"Just the same," Jedidiah replied, "I want to get you over to Doc's office and let him examine you."

After a few attempts of sliding out the loading ramp, which had been wedged in the landing,

Jedidiah and Matthew finally managed to get it lowered. The two of them helped Tom limp across the field and down the streets of Spoon Fork. Sheriff Thompson trailed along with them, waiting to hear the full story and see what he could do to help.

Doc Stone, a tall, grizzled man with sharp eyes and a handlebar mustache that rivaled Phineas B. Hargroves, met them at the door. "Bring him in here," he directed, motioning to an examination table. "What happened?"

"Didn't you get the telegram?" Matthew asked, puzzled. "Phineas said he was going to send it!"

"I did," Doc Stone seemed irritated by the question. "You do realize all it said was that he was injured and needed medical attention, don't you?"

"He was attacked," Jedidiah explained quickly.

"Attacked!" the doctor exploded. "By who?"

"Was it the same person or persons who tried to sabotage your place?" Sheriff Thompson asked.

"Sabotage!" the doctor exclaimed as Tom was helped up onto the examination table. "Look, if the three of you are going to discuss sabotage and other things like that, will you kindly do it somewhere else? I need to concentrate on my patient!"

Jedidiah, Matthew, and Sheriff Thompson all immediately agreed and stepped outside the door.

Sheriff Thompson, sensing his friend's turmoil, placed a reassuring hand on his shoulder. "We'll get to the bottom of this, Jed. But right now, let's focus on making sure Tom is okay."

Jedidiah nodded, his determination renewed. "You're right, Sheriff. We won't let whoever's behind this get away with it."

"But don't you see, Jed," Sheriff Thompson began, "this only goes to show that my concerns were valid. The race is still two weeks away, and the stakes are already higher than ever!"

"I guess you're right," the young ranch owner nodded his head solemnly. "I wasn't taking the rumors as seriously as I should have before, and now Tom is paying the price."

The tension in the air was thick as they waited for the doctor's verdict. Every second felt like an eternity. Finally, the door opened. Tom Miller and Doc Stone stepped outside, smiling and laughing. Despite having a bandage wrapped around his head, Tom seemed to be no worse for wear.

"Is he okay, Doc?" Jedidiah asked anxiously.

"Say, didn't anyone ever tell you that young people have hard heads?" Doc Stone asked with a half smile. "You two should know. I've treated both of you often enough."

"So he's gonna be okay?" Jedidiah asked, relieved.

"Give him a couple of days to rest, and he'll be better than ever!" Doc Stone said reassuringly. "Now if you don't mind, the four of you can leave.

I have real sick patients to attend to!"

"Gladly," Jedidiah laughed, relief washing over him, as he and the others turned to walk away.

As they moved through the streets, Sheriff Thompson glanced over at Jedidiah and said, "I'll have my deputies keep an eye on your ranch. Whoever did this won't get away with it, again."

"I would appreciate that," Davenport replied. "And I'll have my foreman, instruct his men to do the same." Turning to Tom Miller he said, "Don't worry about coming into work tomorrow. Take the next two days off to rest. If you're up to it, come back Wednesday. If not, just let us know and you can have more time off."

The young man started to argue, but the throbbing pain in his head made him realize it might be better if he did take a couple of days off. He reluctantly nodded and accepted his employer's offer.

After Tom had headed home and the sheriff had returned to his office, Jedidiah and Matthew decided to return to the field and survey the damage to the Phoenix.

As they approached the airship, the full extent of the crash's impact became evident. Jedidiah stood in the field, looking it over. The undercarriage was a mess of splintered wood, and the once sleek lines of the airship were marred by the rough landing. His mind flooded with thoughts of the upcoming race.

"It's taken quite a beating," Matthew remarked, his voice filled with concern.

Jedidiah nodded, his expression solemn. "It certainly has and it's going to take a lot of work to get it back in shape." He turned and headed toward the telegraph office. "I'll send a wire to Phineas and have him come take a look."

About an hour later, the eccentric older man came riding into town in one of Jedidiah's buggies. He turned and headed straight toward the site of the crash, his face still flushed with excitement from the recent events.

In the meantime, Jedidiah and Matthew had been busy patching the hole in the airbag. Using heavy canvas and a specialized adhesive designed to withstand high pressure, they worked meticulously to seal the tear. The process required them to heat the adhesive until it became pliable, then apply it evenly over the patch and the surrounding area. They used metal clamps to hold everything in place until it set.

Once the patch was secure, they connected hoses from the airship's emergency gas tanks to refill the airbag. The tanks hissed and vibrated as the mixture of hydrogen and helium was pumped back into the bag. The airship gradually began to lift slightly as the bag refilled, providing just enough buoyancy to make the next steps of the recovery easier.

Phineas, arriving just as they finished, observed their handiwork with approval. "Looks like you've managed to stabilize her, at least for now," he said, nodding towards the patched airbag.

"First things first, I've made out a list of supplies and parts I'll need to repair the Icarus," he said, waving a piece of paper. Jedidiah took the list from Phineas, gave it to Matthew, and asked if he would take care of it.

"Consider it done," Matthew replied, already turning to head toward the freight office to fill out the necessary forms.

As Matthew disappeared from view, Phineas turned to Jedidiah, his brow furrowed. With a look of regret, he said, "My dear boy, I'm afraid there's just no way we can get the repairs done to your ship in time for the race."

"That's what I figured," Jedidiah replied, his tone surprisingly calm. Despite the gravity of the situation, he seemed more composed than Phineas expected.

"You don't seem too worried about missing out on the race," Phineas stated calmly.

Jedidiah smiled a glint of determination in his eyes. "I've got a plan. The Phoenix may be out of commission, but I'm not out of the race." With a devilish grin, he added, "Not yet anyway."

"Are you thinking about entering the Eclipse?"

Phineas asked curiously. "It's not as fast, but with a few modifications, it might just give you a fighting chance."

Jedidiah raised an eyebrow. "The Eclipse? It's a solid ship, but I would have to make a lot of modifications if I wanted to make it ready in time." Then matter-of-factly, he added, "Besides, it's already in steady use at the freight office I just opened in Topeka."

Phineas sighed and shrugged his shoulders. "My dear boy, you have me utterly confused. Your ship is lying in ruins, and yet you're so calm."

Jedidiah clapped him on the back. "Well, my dear professor, it's something you'll just have to find out about in due time." Glancing back at his prized vessel, Davenport added, "In the meantime, we need to figure out how to get the Phoenix back to the ranch."

Phineas nodded, deep in thought. "Flying it back is out of the question. The bottom might fall out completely, causing the entire ship to dismantle in midair."

"What if we towed it back to the ranch?" Jedidiah asked curiously.

Phineas stroked his mustache, pondering the logistics. "We would need something stable enough to support its weight. Perhaps a flatbed wagon. We could hover the Phoenix just high enough to slide a couple of wagons underneath, secure them to the frame, and use mules to pull the whole thing back to the ranch."

Jedidiah's eyes lit up. "That's a brilliant idea, Phineas. The airbag should hold together long enough to provide enough lift to keep the load light. I'll wire Jim Davis to come out with some of the men, a few wagons, and the mules."

Phineas nodded, already thinking through the details. "We'll have to make sure the airship is as secure as possible before moving it. We don't want any further damage during the tow."

Jedidiah agreed. "Sounds great. Let's get started. I'll go ahead and telegraph the ranch. I'll use the one in the freight office. Can you stay here and oversee the operation?"

"Of course," Phineas replied, already starting to analyze the vessel's structural integrity.

Jedidiah joined Matthew in the freight office. The latter had just finished filling out the supply forms. Davenport updated him about the plans to take the Phoenix home.

Within an hour, Jim Davis and a group of ranch hands were ready with the necessary equipment. Once they arrived in town, Jedidiah led the convoy back to the crash site, where Phineas anxiously waited to take command of the mission.

With everyone working together, Jedidiah released the proper mixture of gases into the airbag, lifting the Phoenix just enough to slide the wagons underneath. The boards creaked and the timbers strained, but they held firm. Once the wagons were in place, they carefully attached ropes to secure the airship. Once this was done, they hitched the mules. Phineas looked everything over one last time, ensuring it was ready for the long journey home.

As the convoy began to move, the townsfolk gathered to watch with a mixture of concern and admiration.

The trek back was treacherous, but with careful planning and coordination, they managed to tow the Phoenix back to the ranch without any further incidents. By the time they arrived, the sun was setting, casting a golden glow over the landscape.

Exhausted but relieved, Jedidiah and his team began the process of securing the Phoenix in the hangar, where repairs would eventually begin.

Just as they finished, Jedidiah noticed a figure in the shadows near the door to his workshop. He squinted, trying to make out who it was, but the stranger suddenly made a run for it.

"Matthew," Jedidiah called urgently, "there's someone in here!"

"Where?"

"There!" Davenport shouted as he raced towards the door, with Matthew right behind him. Both men sprinted after the mysterious figure, just as he darted into the woods. The intruder was fast, but Jedidiah and Matthew were determined. They pushed through the underbrush, their breaths coming in ragged gasps as they closed the distance.

"Stop!" Jedidiah shouted, but the fugitive didn't slow down.

As they continued their pursuit of the shadowy figure, Jedidiah and Matthew both tried to catch a glimpse of who they were chasing. There was a brief moment when the moonlight caught his profile, revealing youthful features, but shadowed enough to obscure any details.

Just as they were about to catch up, the mysterious stranger turned and threw something at them. Round metal balls hit the ground, and a thick cloud of smoke filled the air. Jedidiah and Matthew began coughing violently as they stumbled to a halt.

"Where did he go?" Matthew asked, trying to wave the smoke out of his face. He unexpectedly fell to the ground.

"I don't know," Davenport replied, his voice filled with frustration. He gasped for breath as he dropped to his knees and collapsed next to Colton.

CHAPTER VII

Plans and Preparations

After what felt like only a few minutes, Jedidiah Davenport began to regain consciousness. His head was pounding, and his vision was a blur. Slowly, he tried to sit up but felt a wave of dizziness wash over him. Beside him, Matthew Colton groaned as he too began to stir.

"Matt," Jedidiah croaked, his voice barely above a whisper. "You okay?"

Matthew blinked a few times, then nodded weakly. "Yeah, I think so. What happened?"

Jedidiah struggled to remember. The last thing he recalled was chasing the shadowy figure through the woods. "We need to figure out what's going on."

With great effort, the two young men managed to stand. Still reeling from the effects, they stumbled towards the ranch house, the night eerily quiet around them.

As they opened the front door and stepped inside, they spotted Phineas B. Hargroves, Pat Bennington, and Agatha Porter pacing back and forth in the living room, brows furrowed in deep thought. Relief washed over their faces as they spotted Jedidiah and Matthew entering.

Phineas immediately stopped pacing and rushed toward them, his face lighting up, while Pat threw his hands up in the air and exclaimed, "Jumpin' Jehoshaphat! Where have the two of you been?"

"You had us all worried half to death!" Agatha added, crossing her arms across her chest. She glared at them, her worry morphing into irritation now that she knew they were safe. "Are the two of you okay?"

Jedidiah and Matthew exchanged confused looks. "We're fine..." Jedidiah started, his voice tinged with bewilderment. "You act like we've been gone for ages. It's only been a few minutes."

"A few minutes!" Phineas exploded, his eyes wide with exasperation. He threw his hands up in disbelief. "My dear boy, it's been three hours!"

Jedidiah's eyes widened in shock. He quickly reached into his pocket, pulled out his silver watch with the gold-embossed train on the lid, and checked the time. His mouth dropped open.

"Gosh!" Matthew exclaimed, leaning in to get a closer look at Jedidiah's watch. "It *has* been three hours!"

"I don't know what happened," Jedidiah sighed, shaking his head as he replaced the cherished memento. "We were chasing after that mysterious figure, he threw some kind of smoke bomb at us, and that's the last thing we remember."

"Thank goodness you're both alright!" Phineas exclaimed, his shoulders relaxing as he let out a deep breath. "It could have been much worse for the two of you."

"Well," Pat Bennington smiled as he reached into his pocket and pulled out a box of matches, his face breaking into a grin, "I reckon I better set off the found 'em flares!"

"Found 'em flares?" Jedidiah asked, his eyebrows raised in confusion. "Don't you mean rescue flares?"

Pat smirked, shaking his head slightly. "Well, if we were looking to be rescued, then I'd set off the rescue flares," he explained, striking a match. "But since we're letting Jim Davis and the other boys know to call off the search because we found you, we're setting off the..."

"Found 'em flares..." Jedidiah finished his sentence, a small smile playing on his lips.

"Say," Pat laughed, clapping Jedidiah on the shoulder. "You catch on fast! No wonder you're the boss!"

With a serious expression, Davenport said, "Yes, it was my flare expertise that earned me the

Pat Bennington eagerly waited
to set off the *Found 'Em* flares.

title."

After Pat had gone, Agatha retreated to her room to prepare for bed. Once they had left, the atmosphere grew more serious. Phineas B. Hargroves cleared his throat as he regarded the others with a grave expression. "This is more than just sabotage. Someone is trying to derail us entirely, and they don't care how they do it."

Matthew paced the room, his brow furrowed in thought. "We need to tighten security around the ranch even more than we already planned," he stated, glancing at Jedidiah. "No one goes anywhere alone. We need to watch each other's backs at all times!"

Jedidiah nodded, his jaw set with determination. "Agreed. We also need to start repairing the Icarus the moment the supplies arrive. The race is coming up fast, and we can't afford any more setbacks."

Phineas stood up straighter, determination shining in his eyes as he clenched his fists. "I'll start dismantling the engine first thing in the morning. We'll make sure it's in tip-top shape."

Jedidiah crossed his arms, his gaze firm. "And I'll coordinate with Jim Davis to hire some extra hands to patrol the ranch. We're going to need all the help we can get."

The mention of the race gave Matthew a sudden thought. "Wait a minute!" He exclaimed. "What about the Phoenix? We've got to get it in shape too!"

Phineas sighed, rubbing his temples as he reluctantly explained, "I'm afraid, my dear boy, that while not a total loss, the Phoenix will never be ready in time for the race." He glanced over at Jedidiah puzzled and asked, "Did you not explain this to him earlier?"

"No, he didn't!" Matthew retorted. "Somehow he managed to leave that little detail out!" His frustration was evident, his fists clenching at his sides. He turned and looked at his childhood friend for an explanation.

"Unfortunately, Phineas is right," Jedidiah sighed reluctantly. "The Phoenix will fly again, but not anytime soon."

"So that's it!" Matthew exclaimed. "After all that hard work, we're just out of the race?"

Jedidiah's eyes sparkled with a hint of mystery as he replied, "Not exactly."

Matthew's confusion deepened, his eyebrows knitting together. "Not exactly... What do you mean, not exactly? Are you planning to use one of the ships from the freight line?"

"Not exactly..." Jedidiah repeated, a small smile playing on his lips.

Phineas threw his hands up in frustration, his voice tinged with annoyance. "I asked him that earlier and got basically the same response! The lad is being completely obstinate and won't divulge his secret. Obviously, he has something up his sleeve, but he's not telling what it is!"

"You'll both have to trust me," Jedidiah grinned as he continued to remain tight-lipped. Shortly after, everyone reluctantly agreed to drop the subject and retire for the evening.

****

The next morning, as the sun rose in the sky, Jim Davis and his men began setting up a perimeter around the ranch, ready to resume their roles as guardians of the land. The foreman explained the situation and laid out the security plan to his team.

"We'll set up rotating shifts," Jim stated authoritatively. "Keep an eye on all the entrances to the property and make sure no one gets through without us knowing."

He assigned checkpoints and patrols around the property, the atmosphere growing tense as everyone remained determined to ward off potential saboteurs.

Meanwhile, Phineas and Matthew had begun repairs on the Icarus. The damage from the sabotage had been extensive, but guided by Phineas' expertise and relentless determination, they made steady progress.

Jedidiah, however, was nowhere to be seen. He had slipped away that morning after an exceptionally early breakfast, his whereabouts a mystery.

Later in the day, Davenport finally reappeared, having taken a moment to stroll around his ranch. The rolling hills and open skies, usually sources of peace, now seemed fraught with unseen dangers. Taking a deep breath, he prepared himself for what lay ahead.

"Jed!" Matthew called from just outside Phineas' hangar. "We could use an extra pair of hands in here."

Jedidiah turned and made his way over to his friend, but only to explain that he had more pressing matters on his agenda that couldn't wait. As he approached, Matthew adjusted his gun belt and glanced down at the revolver at his side. He didn't normally wear it around the ranch, but with the constant threat of sabotage, he felt it was better not to take any chances.

"Jed, are you sure you shouldn't be more prepared?" Matthew asked, looking up at him. "I know you're disappointed about not being able to enter the Phoenix in the race, but..."

Jedidiah placed a reassuring hand on Matthew's shoulder. "I understand your concern, but don't worry. We'll make it to Wichita, and I have confidence that Phineas will have the Icarus in tip-top shape well before the race."

Glancing down at Matthew's sidearm, he added,

"Carrying that gun right now might cause more tension than it's worth. Jim and the other men have a tight rein on security. Let's try to keep things as calm as possible around here and just concentrate on repairing the Icarus."

Matthew nodded reluctantly. "Alright, but I'll keep it nearby, just in case."

Glancing into the hangar and then back at Jedidiah, Colton said, "Well, if you're not going to help with the repairs, could you at least tell me what you're up to?"

"You'll find out," the young entrepreneur smiled mysteriously as he turned on his heel and walked away, leaving Matthew still feeling a bit uneasy but trusting his friend's judgment.

****

For the next two weeks, the ranch buzzed with activity. All their intense work had finally paid off. The Icarus was repaired, and no one had seen any further signs of sabotage. The day before the race, the atmosphere was charged with anticipation. Phineas B. Hargroves meticulously rechecked everything one last time, while Jedidiah remained conspicuously absent, raising many questions. He hadn't been joining them for meals and routinely returned home after everyone had gone to bed, leaving again before they woke up the next day.

Tom Miller, having recovered from his previous ordeal, rode out to the ranch to offer his assistance. Guiding his horse, Daisy, through the familiar terrain, he felt a mix of determination and apprehension.

Upon arriving, Tom was greeted by the sight of Phineas and Matthew deep in discussion near the Icarus.

"Tom! Good to see you," Matthew called out, waving him over.

"How are you feeling?" Phineas asked, his concern evident.

"I'm much better, thanks," Tom replied with a nod. "I wanted to see if there was anything I could do to help."

Phineas and Matthew exchanged a quick glance before Phineas spoke up. "Actually, there is something you can do. We need someone to stay here and guard the Icarus while we go look for Jed. We can't afford any more sabotage."

Tom nodded, feeling a surge of responsibility. "You can count on me, Mr. Hargroves!"

"My dear boy," the eccentric older man smiled warmly, "How many times have I told you not to call me Mr. Hargroves?" He patted Tom on the shoulder. "Call me *Professor* Hargroves!"

Tom blushed a little from embarrassment. "Oops! Sorry, *Professor* Hargroves."

"Not a problem, my boy," Phineas replied as he

walked away. "We shall return!"

"Thanks, Tom," Matthew said, clapping Tom on the shoulder as he turned to follow the older man.

Matthew mounted his horse, while Phineas climbed aboard his carriage. The two of them rode away, leaving Tom alone in the hangar with the Icarus. The airship loomed above him like a towering giant.

Tom settled into his watch, pacing around the hangar and checking the perimeter. The minutes ticked by slowly, the quiet interrupted only by the occasional rustle of leaves or the distant call of a bird. Tom's thoughts drifted to the gravity of their situation and the determination of their unknown adversary.

Suddenly, a faint noise caught his attention. He turned towards the source and saw a shadowy figure sneaking into the hangar. His heart raced as he recognized the intruder. It was the same person who had bumped into him and knocked him down at the party two weeks ago, the one he had chased into this very hangar before being struck from behind.

With adrenaline surging through his veins, Tom sprang into action. He looked around for a weapon and spotted a large metal wrench leaning against the boarding ramp. Tom picked it up and quietly made his way towards the intruder.

Reflecting on his previous attempt to catch the

fiend, Tom reminded himself not to be caught off guard again. "I have to stay vigilant," he muttered to himself, tightening his grip on the wrench. "I won't let them sabotage us again."

"Stop right there!" Tom shouted, his voice echoing through the building. Startled, the figure turned and bolted for the exit. Tom gave chase, his heart pounding in his chest. They weaved through the ranch, dodging obstacles and pushing through the underbrush.

Despite his best efforts, Tom lost sight of the saboteur as he disappeared into the dense forest. Tom slowed to a stop, panting and frustrated. "Darn it," he muttered, scanning the surroundings for any sign of the figure, but there were none.

Realizing that the intruder could be planning another attack, Tom made a quick decision. "I can't let them get away with this," he thought, his mind racing. "If they strike again during the race, it could be catastrophic. I need to be there to stop them."

With determination, Tom resolved to stow away aboard the Icarus. He determined that he could intervene if trouble arose. The young man was keenly aware of the risks but refused to let his friends down again. With a firm nod, Tom hurried back to the hangar and found a small, concealed compartment in the cargo hold where he could hide.

As he settled into the cramped space, he

whispered to himself, "*Just let them try to sabotage us now!*"

****

Meanwhile, Phineas B. Hargroves and Matthew Colton continued riding the range, searching for any sign of Jedidiah. They called his name, their voices echoing through the quiet valley. After what felt like hours, they finally spotted a lone rider in the distance.

"It's Jedidiah!" Phineas exclaimed, urging the horse to pull his buggy forward.

As they approached, they saw Davenport riding his horse Blaze, a look of calm determination on his face. He reined in his horse as they drew near, a small smile forming on his lips.

"Where have you been, Jed?" Matthew asked, his voice filled with concern and a hint of frustration. "We've been working ourselves to the bone trying to get the Icarus ready, and you just disappear?"

"I had things to do," Jedidiah replied cryptically. His calm demeanor only seemed to aggravate Matthew more.

"Jed," the young man was almost shaking he was so angry. "You do realize the race is tomorrow, don't you? At the very least, you could have checked in on us! Where have you been for the past two weeks?"

"You're absolutely right," Davenport replied apologetically. "I should have. I've just been carried away preparing a surprise."

"Preparing a surprise?" Phineas echoed his tone a mix of curiosity and annoyance. "For two weeks? While we've been out there, dealing with the repercussions of the saboteur and trying to keep everything together?"

Jedidiah's smile faded slightly, and he nodded. "Yeah, I know it seems like I abandoned you, but trust me, what I've been doing is just as important as the work you've been doing."

Matthew dismounted, his face flushed with anger. "Important? We've barely slept, Jed! We've been repairing the Icarus and trying to secure the ranch! You should have been helping us!"

Jedidiah looked between his two friends, seeing the strain and frustration in their eyes. He sighed, knowing he owed them an explanation. "I understand you're upset, and you have every right to be. But what I'm about to show you will explain everything."

Phineas, still sitting on the seat of his buggy, crossed his arms. "My dear boy, this better be good. We've been on edge for weeks."

Jedidiah nodded solemnly and led them down a winding path through the ranch. The tension in the air was thick with unspoken words and lingering frustration. After a while, they arrived at a secluded valley hidden from view by the surrounding hills. There, nestled among the trees, was a large newly constructed hangar that neither Phineas nor Matthew had ever seen before.

"This is it," Jedidiah said, dismounting and leading them inside.

Inside the hangar, their eyes widened in amazement, and they both gasped at what they saw. There, gleaming under the soft light, was an airship unlike any they had ever seen. Sleek and streamlined, it looked built for speed and agility.

"This," Jedidiah said proudly, "is the Swift!"

CHAPTER VIII

The Journey Begins

"The Swift!" Matthew Colton exclaimed excitedly, completely forgetting that he had just been furious with his friend a moment earlier. "Gosh! It's a beaut!" He ran his eyes up and down the sleek lines of the newly constructed airship with pride and admiration.

Phineas slowly approached the vessel, his eyes more critical. "Incredible... Did you build an entire airship without me? How long have you been working on this?"

Jedidiah smiled, running a hand along the polished surface of the Swift. "For almost three months. I wanted to surprise you both, but more importantly, I wanted to ensure I had something truly unique. The Swift incorporates everything I've learned from the Icarus, the Phoenix, the Navigator, the Eclipse, and the Drifter."

"For almost three months?" Phineas repeated,

his voice tinged with a mix of disbelief and disappointment. "That means you must have started on it immediately after we cleared up all that nasty business with the railroad."

"Pretty much," Jedidiah replied. "I hired some men from Hawthorn Grove to work on it in secret. While they were constructing the hangar, I started the designs for the Swift."

Phineas fell silent for a moment, his gaze shifting from the airship to Jedidiah. "I have to admit," he began slowly, "I'm a bit hurt you didn't include me on this project. We've always worked on these things together."

"Well, for one, you were too busy overseeing the construction of my other ships for the freight company," Jedidiah explained. "I didn't want to pull you away from those projects. Besides, I wanted to build this one on my own. I wanted it to be my own design. I planned from the start to enter this ship in the race, so I wanted it to be special."

Phineas took a deep breath, his frustration slowly giving way to understanding. "Well, I suppose that makes sense," he conceded, his voice softening. He walked around the Swift, taking in its sleek design. "It's... it's really something, Jed."

Phineas suddenly looked up as though a thought had just struck him. "You had planned to enter this ship in the race the whole time? That's why when Myra said she saw your name on the full registration list, it didn't mention the Phoenix. It merely read, Jedidiah Davenport and his Airship!"

Jedidiah smiled and nodded. "That's exactly why. This is the biggest secret I've ever kept!"

"That's amazing, Jed." Matthew beamed. However, his smile temporarily faded as he crossed his arms and began to look skeptical. "But why did you keep it a secret for so long?"

Jedidiah's eyes met Matthew's, his expression earnest. "Because I needed to be sure it was perfect. This race isn't just about winning; it's about proving what we can achieve. I didn't want to reveal it until I was confident it was ready. And with all the sabotage attempts, I couldn't risk anyone discovering it."

Phineas nodded, his respect for Jedidiah growing. He finally allowed a small smile to break through. "It's beautiful," he said, his voice filled with admiration. "My dear boy, you've outdone yourself. This will truly be a game-changer." He smiled as he clapped Davenport on the shoulder and added, "And to think, I was worried that you weren't taking this race very seriously. I thought that you had just given up and weren't going to be competing at all!"

Phineas glanced back at the speediest airship he had ever seen and said, "But don't think just because you've created this beauty that I'm going to count myself out of the race. I plan to give you a run for your money like you've never seen before!"

Jedidiah smiled gratefully. "Thank you, Phineas. And again, I'm sorry for the secrecy. I know you both have every right to be upset with me."

Phineas nodded, his expression softening further. "My dear boy, think no more of it. Now, if it is all right with you, I'd like to take a look around the inside. Even though I didn't design it, maybe I can offer some little tips.

Jedidiah nodded. "I'd appreciate that, Phineas. Your expertise is always welcome."

The three men spent the next couple of hours going over every detail of the Swift, ensuring that everything was in top condition. Phineas's critical eye and expert knowledge helped identify and address a few minor issues, making the Swift even more race-ready.

Finally, with nothing left to inspect, Phineas stepped back and proudly announced, "All systems are go!"

Jedidiah nodded, his heart swelling with pride. "Thank you, Phineas. Let's get it out in the open."

"I'm afraid I can't take it out for a test flight with you," Phineas reluctantly replied. "I've got a few more things to pack for the trip. Never can be too prepared, you know!"

Jedidiah completely understood and told his friend he'd meet him at the field and they could travel to Wichita together.

After Phineas had gone, Jedidiah moved to a control panel near the side of the hangar. The panel was an intricate device, a blend of brass levers and dials, all connected to the small steam-powered generator that powered the hangar's roof. With practiced precision, Jedidiah pulled a lever, and the generator hummed to life.

The sound of gears and pistons filled the air as the massive roof of the hangar began to open. The two large halves creaked and groaned as they slowly parted, revealing the clear blue sky above. Sunlight poured into the hangar, bathing the Swift in a warm, golden glow.

"That's always impressive," Matthew remarked, shading his eyes as he looked up at the opening roof.

After it fully opened, Jedidiah turned to Matthew and said. "Alright, let's get going!" His voice tinged with excitement.

Before boarding the airship, Jedidiah and Matthew tied their horses securely to a nearby rail, planning to send a couple of ranch hands for them later.

Moments later, they were standing on the deck of the Swift. The airship's engines roared to life, a deep, resonant sound that echoed through the hangar. Jedidiah pulled a few levers that detached the mooring lines, and the sleek vessel began to rise.

The massive propellers spun slowly, creating a powerful downdraft that stirred up dust and debris on the hangar floor. The Swift lifted gracefully, its sleek form cutting through the air with ease. Jedidiah's hands moved deftly over the controls, guiding the airship as it ascended.

"Here we go," Jedidiah murmured, as the Swift cleared the top of the hangar and hovered in the open sky. The feeling of the ship responding perfectly to his commands was exhilarating, a testament to the countless hours of work and meticulous planning. The ranch below began to shrink as they gained altitude.

"It's flying beautifully," Matthew called out from his station, his voice filled with excitement.

The airship hovered for a moment, adjusting to the open air. Jedidiah's heart continued to swell with pride as he guided the Swift further away from the hangar, feeling the thrill of this maiden voyage. The engines hummed with perfect harmony.

"Let's take it for a spin around the ranch before we meet up with Phineas," Jedidiah suggested enthusiastically. Matthew eagerly agreed.

As the Swift climbed higher, Jedidiah steered it towards the northwestern part of the ranch, where his recently discovered oil deposit lay. From this vantage point, the sprawling expanse of Davenport Ranch unfolded beneath him, a patchwork of verdant fields and rolling hills. The wind rushed past, carrying the scent of fresh earth and the promise of adventure.

Soon, the machinery of the oil field came into view. Below, a network of derricks and pumps dotted the landscape, their skeletal frames stark against the green backdrop. The steam-powered engines that drove the pumps chugged rhythmically, their metal arms rising and falling in a tireless dance to extract the precious oil from the earth. Each pumpjack, with its distinctive horse-head design, bobbed methodically.

Massive wooden storage tanks stood nearby, their surfaces weathered but sturdy, connected by a labyrinth of pipes that snaked across the ground. Workers moved with practiced efficiency, tending to the machinery and ensuring everything operated smoothly. The hiss of steam and the clank of metal echoed up to the Swift, a symphony of industry that underscored the significance of this discovery.

Jedidiah looked down at the bustling activity, a sense of satisfaction settling over him. The oil deposit had transformed his ranch, providing the financial backbone for his ambitious projects. It had enabled him to build the Swift, along with his other ships.

As he watched the machinery working tirelessly, his mind drifted back to that pivotal moment on Wednesday, May 18th, 1881, when

A network of derricks and pumps dotted
the landscape, their skeletal frames stark
against the green backdrop.

they had first discovered the oil.

****

They had been searching for any sign of what could have driven Elijah Perkins of the D.&R.W. Railroad to covet Jedidiah's land so intensely. After hours of fruitless searching near the exit of the secret tunnel, frustration had set in. But then, as they were about to call it a day, Matthew had fallen through a hidden opening in a dense patch of brush. He landed in a shallow pool of dark, pungent liquid.

"What's all this stuff?" Matthew had asked, bewildered, looking down at his soaked boots and pants. Jedidiah climbed down and joined him; the strong odor filled the air. The realization hit him with a jolt—Matthew was sitting in oil. They had discovered a natural seep on his property. This was what Perkins had been after the whole time.

****

With a deep breath, Jedidiah turned his gaze back to the horizon. The Swift responded to his touch, banking smoothly as it set its course to rendezvous with Phineas.

As Jedidiah and Matthew maneuvered the Swift back toward the main field, the activity on the ranch became more visible. Workers and ranch hands, going about their usual duties, began to look up, their expressions turning to surprise and awe as they spotted the new, unfamiliar airship approaching.

Phineas had returned and moved the Icarus outside of its hangar. It was sitting moored in the open field, gleaming in the sunlight, ready for its own journey. The older man looked up as the Swift approached, a mixture of pride and competitive spirit evident on his face.

As the Swift descended and landed next to the other vessel, the gathered crowd grew silent, their faces reflecting a mix of shock and curiosity. Jedidiah felt a swell of pride at the sight of his friends and workers, all of whom had contributed in their way to this moment, even if they hadn't known it. The airship touched down smoothly. Jedidiah and Matthew immediately disembarked to join the others.

Phineas approached, extending his hand. "Well done, my dear boy. Well done indeed."

Jedidiah shook his hand firmly. "Thank you, Phineas. I couldn't have done it without everything I've learned from you."

Phineas nodded, then looked at both airships. "It's time to show the world what we can do. Ready to head to Wichita?"

"Ready as ever," Jedidiah replied, a determined

glint in his eye. He motioned for a few ranch hands to retrieve his and Matthew's luggage from inside the hangar housing the Phoenix and load them aboard the Swift.

After this was taken care of, Jedidiah motioned for everyone else to come closer. The workers and ranch hands gathered in a semi-circle. Jedidiah stepped forward, raising his hands to quiet the murmurs.

"Friends, I want to take a moment to thank each and every one of you. Your hard work and dedication have made everything we're about to do possible. This ranch and all its success are a testament to your unwavering efforts."

The crowd erupted into applause, their faces beaming with pride.

Jedidiah continued, "While we're away, Jim Davis will be in charge and keeping an eye on everything."

Jim Davis, standing tall and proud, nodded firmly. "You got it, Jed. You can count on me. I promise to keep things running smoothly and make sure no trouble comes our way."

The crowd murmured their agreement, feeling reassured by Jim's leadership.

Pat Bennington, standing next to Agatha Porter, couldn't resist a playful jab. He puffed out his chest and said, "Don't worry, Jed. I'll personally put myself in charge of making sure Agatha here keeps the house in order."

Agatha crossed her arms, giving Pat a mock stern look. "Oh, is that so? And who's going to keep *you* in order? Someone has to make sure you don't sneak off with all the 'extra' pies you always bake. They're supposed to be for the ranch hands." She turned and looked around at the others and said, "But I've noticed none of you ever seem to get them."

Pat chuckled, patting his round belly. "I promise to leave at least one tin for everyone else. Maybe."

Agatha rolled her eyes. "Well, to be on the safe side, I'll be making daily checks of that broom closet you usually stash them in."

Pat's eyes grew wide as he realized that Agatha knew about his secret hiding place. "That's why all the rhubarb pies keep disappearing!"

Agatha adjusted the bun on top of her head and with the most dignified look on her face replied, "I can't help it if those happen to be my favorite."

The crowd laughed, the light-hearted exchange easing some of the tension.

Jedidiah, smiling at the comical banter, called out, "Alright, everyone, it's time for us to head out. We've got a race to win!"

Before they boarded their vessels, Phineas approached Jedidiah, carrying two leather satchels attached to harnesses.

"Jed, take these," he said, thrusting the packs

into his friend's hands. "These are my latest inventions. They're sort of an improvement on similar existing devices. After that incident on Founder's Day when I was thrown from the Icarus, I decided we couldn't go without them any longer."

Jedidiah looked at the backpacks, his brow furrowing slightly. "What are they?"

Phineas gave a vague smile. "Think of them as a precaution. I'll explain how to use them properly when we have more time, but trust me, you'll want these with you. Especially if the day ever comes and we have to abandon ship mid-flight."

Still slightly confused but trusting his friend's judgment, Jedidiah nodded. "Alright, I'll keep them on the deck next to the rail. Thanks, Phineas."

The engines of the Swift and the Icarus roared to life, filling the air with a powerful hum. The crowd stepped back, watching in awe as they prepared for takeoff.

The two majestic vessels began rising steadily into the sky. The Swift, with its sleek, cutting-edge design, and the Icarus, with its more basic and familiar design, ascended together.

As they climbed higher, the ranch below began to shrink, the workers waving and cheering them on. Jedidiah took one last look at the land that had given him so much before turning his focus forward. The journey to Wichita and the upcoming race awaited, full of challenges and opportunities.

The two airships sailed away, their destinations set and their spirits high. The challenges ahead were unknown, but with their combined determination and skill, they were ready to face whatever came their way.

As they left the boundaries of the ranch, a sense of accomplishment and anticipation filled Jedidiah's heart. He glanced over at the Icarus. He could see Phineas, who was smiling broadly, the wind tousling his hair. Everything seemed perfect.

Unbeknownst to them, on a distant hillside overlooking the ranch, two burly men sat on horseback, watching the airships with keen interest. One of the men, the same one who had attacked Phineas in his hotel room a few months prior and then again at the Founder's Day celebration, held a rifle identical to the one Jedidiah had created, with the enhanced scope and range finder.

He lifted the weapon to his shoulder and focused his sights through the viewfinder. The crosshairs settled squarely on Phineas B. Hargroves. The man's finger hovered over the trigger, a wicked grin spreading across his face. He took a deep breath and prepared to pull the trigger. Barely a moment later, the deafening sound of a gunshot filled the air!

CHAPTER IX

The Night Before the Race

The gunshot echoed across the open landscape, startling birds from the nearby trees. The sound reverberated in Jedidiah's ears, sending a chill down his spine. He glanced over at Matthew, his heart pounding with fear and confusion.

"Did you hear that?" Matthew shouted, his voice filled with alarm.

Jedidiah nodded, gripping the controls tightly. "I did. Are you okay?"

"I'm fine!" Matthew's eyes widened as realization struck. "What about Phineas?

The two young men immediately turned their gaze towards the Icarus. They both breathed a sigh of relief as they saw Phineas alive and well. However, his demeanor was visibly agitated. Jedidiah and Matthew lowered their goggles and adjusted the lenses to get a better view of what was happening.

Phineas was frantically waving at them and motioning towards his ship's wheel. One of the handles was missing, clearly shot off. He gestured urgently for them to climb higher and keep moving.

Jedidiah's mind raced. Someone had just tried to kill Phineas! Anger and fear surged through him. Who would do such a thing? Was the race really that important? The deep rumble of the Swift's engines filled his ears as he adjusted the valves, feeling the vibrations under his fingers.

The Swift began to ascend, the wind whipping around them, carrying the chill of the higher altitude. As they climbed into the clouds, the landscape below blurred, the familiar shapes of the ranch and fields shrinking below them. Jedidiah pushed forward on the throttle, the engine responding with increased power, putting more distance between them and the ranch.

On the hillside, the man with the rifle cursed. "Briggs, you made me miss!" His eyes glinted with hatred as he turned towards the other man, leaning forward in his saddle. The cool wind rustled the dry grass, carrying the distant sounds of the airships' engines. "How dare you hit the barrel just as I was about to fire!"

"Dawson, you should be thanking me!" Briggs retorted, his voice steady. "We were only supposed to slow them down and take them out of the race." His horse shifted nervously beneath him. "You might be okay with ending up at the end of a rope, but not me!"

The first man holstered his rifle, glaring at Briggs, his hand hovering near his revolver. "Next time you get in my way, I might just forget that you saved my life during the war."

Choosing to ignore the threat and not be intimidated, Briggs replied, "Let's just get moving before they realize where the shot came from! We've got to meet up with Blake and Carter anyway."

The two men spurred their horses and galloped away, leaving behind the faint smell of gunpowder and the echo of Dawson's failed attempt.

Back on the Icarus, Phineas blamed himself for not being more vigilant. They couldn't afford to let their guard down. His hands trembled slightly as he took hold of the damaged wheel.

Aboard the Swift, Jedidiah's thoughts raced. "*What if that shot had hit Phineas? What if there are more of them out there?*" The fear gnawed at him, but he pushed it aside, focusing on the task ahead. Turning to Matthew Colton, he said firmly, "We need to reach Wichita as quickly as possible. And we all need to stay alert. Someone is still trying to stop us, and they won't hesitate to try again."

Matthew nodded in agreement. "We'll get there, Jed. Don't worry!" Despite his own reassurance,

Briggs and Dawson engaged in a heated argument as the Icarus was flying away.

Matthew couldn't shake the unease lingering from the gunshot. He glanced over his shoulder, the memory fresh in his mind. His pulse quickened, and he instinctively reached for his gun, only to remember it wasn't with him. Jedidiah had convinced him to leave it behind, but now Matthew was regretting that decision.

As the Swift and the Icarus continued to ascend higher, leaving the immediate danger below, the air grew colder and thinner, and the clouds enveloped them like a protective cloak. Jedidiah, Matthew, and Phineas remained vigilant, their eyes scanning the skies and horizon, determined not to be caught off guard again.

****

Hours later, as the sun began to set, the sprawling city of Wichita came into view. The sight of the bustling metropolis brought a wave of relief. They had finally arrived.

"We made it," Matthew said, his voice filled with a mix of relief and anticipation. "We did it, Jed."

Jedidiah nodded, a small smile forming on his lips. "We did."

The two airships descended towards the city, their presence drawing the attention of onlookers below. The streets of Wichita were alive with activity, the celebration for tomorrow's race evident in the decorations and crowds. In a field just outside of the city limits, they spotted four other airships, one they instantly recognized as belonging to Myra Wilhemenia Bancroft.

As the Swift and the Icarus approached their designated landing areas, they were greeted by a flurry of excitement and curiosity. Jedidiah expertly guided the Swift to a smooth landing, the engines purring softly as the vessel came to a stop. He exchanged a knowing glance with Matthew, as Phineas landed the Icarus beside them.

After they had all disembarked, a group of officials and spectators rushed forward to greet them. Among them was Mr. Benjamin Thompson, the race coordinator, his face beaming with enthusiasm.

"Welcome to Wichita, gentlemen!" he exclaimed, shaking their hands vigorously. "We're thrilled to have you here. We've heard great things about the two of you and your airships, the Icarus and the Phoenix."

"Thank you," Jedidiah replied, his smile polite. "But I didn't bring the Phoenix with me. I've built an entirely new ship that I'll be entering into the race, the Swift."

Thompson's eyes flickered with curiosity as he asked. "The Swift? What happened to your other ship? The one I've read so much about."

Phineas stepped forward, his expression grave. "An attempt of sabotage," he explained, "Perpetrated against both ships, but the Phoenix was the one that suffered the most."

"Sabotage!" The crowd reacted with murmurs of shock and concern as news of the vandalism spread quickly.

Thompson's expression hardened with resolve. "You're not alone in facing such underhanded tactics. Each contestant here has encountered their own share of skulduggery. We've significantly bolstered security around all airships. No one will approach them without proper authorization."

Jedidiah nodded gratefully. "Thank you, Mr. Thompson. We appreciate the assurance."

"In the meantime," Mr. Thompson motioned towards the Grand Imperial Hotel, the same venue where Jedidiah and Phineas had met a few months prior.

"If you'd like to meet your competitors," Thompson continued, his voice carrying a tone of invitation, "we're currently hosting a banquet in the dining room of the hotel for all the contestants."

"Gosh, that sounds good to me!" Matthew Colton's eyes lit up as he enthusiastically accepted the invitation.

Phineas and Jedidiah exchanged hesitant glances, considering the security of their ships.

"Thank you, Mr. Thompson," Jedidiah replied

calmly, his voice steady. "But I think it would be better if we stayed here to make sure nothing else happens."

Thompson nodded understandingly, but reassured them, "Your ships will be perfectly fine. Marshal Cromwell is personally overseeing the security of all entries. He and his deputies are patrolling the area as we speak. So, fret not, my friends!"

"What do you say?" Jedidiah looked to the eccentric older man to make the final call.

Phineas deliberated for a moment, then smiled wryly. "My dear boy, I think I'll leave the decision up to you!"

Jedidiah chuckled softly, turning to Matthew. "Well, Matt, it looks like it's your call."

Everyone stared at the young man as he thought it over. Matthew grinned at the attention. After a thoughtful moment, he turned back to Mr. Thompson. "Where do we wash up and what time do we eat?"

Everyone burst into laughter as the race coordinator clapped Matthew on the shoulder approvingly. "Good choice! I'm glad you'll be joining us. We'll go over the race route and rules, and like I said, you'll get a chance to meet your fellow competitors."

As they entered the lobby, they were greeted by yet another flurry of activity. Contestants, officials, and spectators mingled with animated enthusiasm. Jedidiah and Matthew noticed a small stand selling postcards and other memorabilia. They picked up a few, admiring the images.

"Hey, look at this," Matthew said, showing a postcard to Jedidiah. "They used the photo from the convention a few months ago. There's the Icarus hovering above the hotel."

Jedidiah smiled. "Phineas, you're going to get a kick out of this."

Phineas B. Hargroves seemed quite amused as he stared at the image. "That was rather cheeky of them. I wish they had consulted me before using the likeness of my vessel." He turned to the clerk and said, "I'll take two dozen copies."

Jedidiah Davenport and Matthew Colton laughed as they exchanged a knowing glance.

As they continued through the lobby, Jedidiah spotted a newspaper on a nearby table. He picked it up and unfolded it, his eyes catching a headline that piqued his interest.

"*Lady Seraphina Blackwood Revealed as Financial Backer of the Race,*" the headline read. Jedidiah scanned the article quickly. It described Lady Seraphina Blackwood as a noblewoman with a passion for innovation and adventure. She had funded numerous explorations and had a keen interest in new technologies. An anonymous source had revealed her as the one fronting the money for the event.

"Interesting," Jedidiah muttered, folding the newspaper and tucking it under his arm. "Seems like this race is more prestigious than I realized."

"Perhaps that's why the entry fee was so steep," Phineas remarked.

"Maybe so," Jedidiah replied thoughtfully, "but all the entries together still aren't enough to cover the prize money for the winner. I've heard rumors it's quite substantial."

They paid for their items and left the lobby. In the dining room, long tables were laden with an array of dishes, from roasted meats to fresh vegetables and baked goods. The warm glow of chandeliers illuminated the room, casting a golden light over the assembled guests.

Jedidiah and Phineas were shown to a table where other contestants were already seated. Among them was one familiar face, Myra Wilhelmina Bancroft, who greeted them with a nod and a smile. Matthew was led to another table designated for crew members rather than captains. Oddly, he was the only one seated there.

"Good to see you all made it," Myra said, her eyes twinkling with curiosity. "I heard about the sabotage. It's a relief to see you here in one piece."

Jedidiah nodded solemnly. "It was a close call."

As they took their seats in front of the place cards with their names on them, Jedidiah noticed the other contestants at the table. Captain Jonathan "Jack" Braddock, a tall man with a rugged demeanor and a confident smirk, leaned back in his chair, arms crossed.

"Glad to see you could join us," Jack said, his voice carrying a hint of challenge. "I was beginning to think you wouldn't make it."

Professor Thaddeus Montgomery, a distinguished-looking man with spectacles and a meticulously groomed beard, nodded politely. "Indeed. Sabotage is a serious matter. It's good to see you unharmed."

Sir Reginald "Reggie" Fortescue, a former military commander with a stoic expression and a stiff posture, added, "We've all faced challenges to get here. It seems someone doesn't want this race to happen."

Jedidiah exchanged a knowing glance with Phineas.

"Yes, but we're here now, and we're ready to compete." He leaned forward, addressing the table. "Mr. Thompson mentioned that each of you has experienced sabotage. What happened to your ships?"

Jack Braddock was the first to speak, his tone casual but with an edge of frustration. "Someone tampered with my coal supply. Stole the entire shipment. Caught it just in time, but it set me back a few days waiting for a new supply."

Thaddeus Montgomery nodded, his expression serious. "I had crucial navigation instruments go missing. Thought it was a mistake at first, but after the third disappearance, it was clear someone was trying to cripple my chances."

Reggie Fortescue's face tightened with anger. "My airship's rudder was sabotaged. We caught it during a routine check. Could have been catastrophic if we hadn't found it in time."

Jedidiah exchanged another glance with Phineas before speaking. "It sounds like whoever is behind this is trying to level the playing field—or worse, eliminate the competition entirely. We need to be on high alert."

Myra Wilhelmina Bancroft leaned in, her voice low. "I've had my fair share of issues too. Someone tampered with the gas lines on the Enigma. Caught it just in time. My entire ship could have gone up in flames!"

Jack Braddock nodded in agreement. "It's clear that someone's targeting us. We need to stick together and share any suspicious activity. If we can figure out who's behind this, we can put a stop to it."

Thaddeus Montgomery adjusted his spectacles again. "Perhaps we should form a pact to watch out for each other and share any intelligence we gather. This race is important, but our safety is paramount."

Reggie Fortescue raised his glass in agreement. "A pact it is, then. We'll keep each other informed and stay vigilant."

The group nodded in agreement, each of them understanding the gravity of the situation. Despite being competitors, they recognized the need to unite against a common threat.

Jedidiah leaned back, feeling a sense of solidarity. "Let's make sure this race is remembered for our achievements, not the sabotage. Together, we'll get to the bottom of this."

Before more could be said, Mr. Thompson stood at the head of the room, tapping a glass to get everyone's attention. "Ladies and gentlemen, welcome to Wichita! We are thrilled to have such a distinguished group of aviators and innovators here for this year's race. Despite the challenges you have each faced, your perseverance and dedication are truly inspiring."

Mr. Thompson paused long enough to pull the cloth off a large object placed on the table next to him. He unveiled a gleaming 16-inch statue for all to see. The room fell silent as the light reflected off its polished surfaces. The statue was an intricate brass figure of a falcon, adorned with a copper top hat and a steel monocle, exuding an air of elegance.

"Feast your eyes on this beauty," Mr. Thompson began, his voice filled with pride. He reached over and lifted the bird up to give everyone a better view. "This solid brass statue, with its copper hat and steel monocle, will be awarded to the winner of our grand race. It symbolizes not only victory but also the spirit of innovation and adventure that each of you embodies."

He paused once again allowing the contestants to admire the craftsmanship. After setting the nearly forty-pound statue back down with a thud, he said, "At each checkpoint along the race, you will be given a miniature version of this statue as proof that you have been there. These checkpoints are strategically located in New York, Toronto, London, and Paris."

Mr. Thompson gestured to three much smaller versions of the statue on the table surrounding it. "In New York, you'll receive a small stamped wooden box to store your miniature collectibles. In Toronto, you'll be awarded a solid steel replica. In London, a solid copper model. And in Paris, a solid brass figure. Collect all these tokens to prove your journey and secure your place in history."

He then smiled broadly and announced, "In addition to this magnificent statue, the winner will also receive a prize of one hundred thousand dollars, a sum worthy of the daring and ingenuity required to win this race."

At the mention of the prize money, the room erupted in thunderous applause and cheers. Contestants exchanged excited glances, some even whistling in amazement. The added incentive of a substantial monetary reward electrified the atmosphere, leaving everyone even more eager to prove their mettle and claim the ultimate victory. Animated conversations filled the room as they all began discussing their strategies and aspirations for the race.

Once they had finally quieted down again, Thompson's gaze swept the room. "Now, friends, this race is not just a test of speed and skill, but a celebration of human ingenuity and the spirit of adventure. Let us all raise a toast, and may the best airship win!"

The room echoed with cheers and the clinking of glasses as everyone raised their drinks.

Myra leaned in, her voice low. "So, any idea who might be behind the sabotage?"

Jedidiah shook his head. "No, but whoever it is, they're determined to stop us. We need to stay on our toes, that's for sure."

Jack Braddock chuckled, his eyes gleaming with a competitive spark. "Well, if they think they can scare me off, they clearly don't know who they're dealing with."

Thaddeus Montgomery adjusted his spectacles, a thoughtful look on his face. "They won't know what hit them if they continue to mess with me!"

Reggie Fortescue was just about to speak when there was a sudden commotion as Marshal

Cromwell and three of his deputies burst into the room, forcibly dragging a young man behind them.

"We've caught the saboteur!" Marshal Cromwell announced, beaming with pride.

CHAPTER X

The Race Begins

Marshal Cromwell's voice echoed through the room, instantly silencing the lively chatter. All eyes turned toward the group of lawmen and their captive. The young man struggled against their grip, his face hidden behind the deputies who were containing him.

Phineas B. Hargroves, Jedidiah Davenport, and the other contestants stood up, straining to catch a glimpse of the young man's face, but it was nearly impossible.

"We heard strange noises coming from the cargo hold of Hargroves' ship, the Icarus," Marshal Cromwell declared, his voice firm. "When we investigated, we found this young scoundrel hiding down there."

Phineas stepped forward, his eyes narrowing as he continued to try to get a look at the vandal. "Strange noises, you say? And you found him in my ship?"

The young man's heart pounded in his chest as the deputies' grips tightened on his arms. He struggled, his mind racing with panic and confusion. "Wait! It's not what you think! I'm not the saboteur!" he shouted, his voice breaking with desperation.

Immediately recognizing his voice, Jedidiah pushed through the crowd. "Marshal, let me see him," he demanded, his voice tinged with urgency.

Reluctantly, the deputies stepped aside, revealing the captive's face. Jedidiah's eyes widened in recognition. "Tom! What are you doing here?"

Phineas, now equally shocked, took a step back. "Tom Miller? Why on earth were you hiding in the Icarus?"

Tom, still being held by the deputies, looked pleadingly at his employer and Professor Hargroves. "I swear, I wasn't trying to sabotage anything! I was trying to help keep it safe."

"Keep it safe?" Jedidiah asked curiously.

"While guarding the Icarus for Mr. Hargroves and Mr. Colton, I spotted someone trying to sneak into the hangar. I chased them but they got away!" He paused to catch his breath before continuing, "So, I came back and hid in the cargo hold in case they or anyone else tried to cause trouble for you along the way."

Marshal Cromwell, clearly taken aback by the revelation, glanced between Tom and the other men. "I take it you know this boy, Professor Hargroves? Mr. Davenport?"

Jedidiah nodded, his mind racing to connect the dots. "Yes, Marshal. Tom works for me. If he says he was trying to protect the ship, I believe him."

Phineas, regaining his composure, addressed the marshal. "It's true. Young Tom here is no saboteur. This was just some big misunderstanding." The eccentric older man reached over and clasped Tom on the shoulder, causing the deputies to loosen their grips. "In fact, I intended to invite Mr. Miller here to come along as my assistant and navigator." He turned and looked at Jedidiah. "Isn't that right, Jed?"

Jedidiah was slightly surprised but decided to play along and nodded in agreement. "That's right," he said, "Phineas told me so himself!"

Marshal Cromwell frowned. "Alright, Mr. Miller. You're free to go, but next time, speak up sooner. We're all on edge, and we can't afford any misunderstandings."

Tom's shoulders slumped, a mixture of relief and lingering fear evident in his eyes. "I panicked. I thought if I revealed myself, you'd think I was mixed up in the sabotage. I didn't want to cause more trouble for Mr. Davenport or Mr. Hargroves."

"Professor, my dear boy," Phineas quickly

corrected him, "Professor."

The tension in the room began to ease as the crowd processed the explanation. Myra Wilhelmina Bancroft stepped forward, her eyes softening as she looked at Tom. "He deserves our thanks, not our suspicion. After all, he was only trying to help!"

"I've already said he was free to go," Marshal Cromwell retorted defensively. He turned to Tom and reiterated, "This could have all been avoided if he had just spoken up"

Tom nodded vigorously, rubbing his wrists where the deputies had gripped him. "I understand, Marshal and I'm sorry for the confusion."

Jedidiah placed a reassuring hand on Tom's shoulder. "It's alright, Tom. We know your intentions were good.

Phineas began to chuckle as he said, "Well, that certainly explains why you were nowhere to be seen when I returned to the hangar."

He smiled warmly and added, "Your dedication is truly remarkable, and I was serious about the offer to bring you aboard as my assistant and navigator for the race." The eccentric older man paused briefly. "That is, if you'd be interested in accepting the job."

Tom's eyes widened, his face lighting up. "Would I!" he exclaimed. "Professor Hargroves, I'd be honored!" He couldn't contain his excitement, letting out a small cheer. "Yahoo!"

As the tension in the room dissipated, Mr. Thompson clapped his hands to regain everyone's attention. He motioned for a server to lead Tom to the table where Matthew Colton was sitting alone and to bring him a plate. Then, he addressed the rest of the crowd.

"Well, now that we've cleared that up, let's get back to our preparations. The race is still on, and we have much to do!"

The room buzzed with renewed energy as the contestants and their crews resumed their discussions. Matthew, who had been anxiously watching from a distance, let out a sigh of relief. "Glad to see you're alright, Tom. We had no idea you had stowed away in Phineas' ship."

Tom smiled, though still a bit shaken. "Thanks, Matt. I guess I really should have told you what I was up to, but I was afraid you would say no and not let me come."

"Chances are good we would have done just that," Matthew laughed. "But now that you're here, we're glad to have you. I'm sure you'll be a great help to Phineas."

Tom suddenly smirked. "And I think it's a much better use of my time than playing errand boy for Mr. Benson back at the freight office."

Matthew Colton laughed as he shook his head. "Yeah, I guess it is," he said.

As the evening progressed, the contestants

continued sharing their concerns about the upcoming race. Despite their recent scares, they were all determined to push ahead, fully understanding the stakes and dangers.

After the banquet, each contestant was given a key to the room they would be staying in overnight. However, both Phineas B. Hargroves and Jedidiah Davenport declined their keys and chose to sleep aboard their ships instead.

"That's not a bad idea!" Myra remarked as she also gave her key back to Mr. Thompson. "Security is great, but there's nothing like the personal touch and doing things yourself to make sure it's done right!"

Professor Thaddeus Montgomery, Sir Reginald Fortescue, and Captain Jonathan Braddock all agreed and did the same.

Shortly after, they all retired to their respective vessels. The night was calm, but tension hung in the air. Deputy marshals continued taking turns patrolling the area, their eyes scanning the shadows for any sign of trouble.

Around midnight, a faint noise stirred Jedidiah from his light sleep. He quickly grabbed a lantern and stepped outside the Swift. He saw Phineas and Myra doing the same, the older man's face a mask of alertness. Jedidiah and Phineas exchanged a nod and split up to check the perimeter.

It turned out to be a false alarm—a stray cat

knocking over some crates. Both men sighed in relief but remained on high alert for the rest of the night.

As Jedidiah was reboarding the Swift, he suddenly overheard a conversation between the two eccentric older airship captains.

"Myra," Phineas nodded curtly, crossing his arms and tilting his head slightly.

"Phineas," she replied sharply, her eyes narrowing as she squared her shoulders.

"Your ship looks adequate," Phineas remarked, glancing over at the Enigma with a dismissive wave of his hand.

Myra took an equally disdainful look at the Icarus, her lip curling slightly. "And yours doesn't look like it will fall apart before we reach the finish line."

"Thank you…" Phineas' eyes widened, his face flushing with sudden anger, "Fall apart! What does that mean?" He suddenly realized how loudly he was speaking and lowered his voice, leaning in closer. "Have you arranged some type of accident for the Icarus? Did you plan for it to fall apart just as we're approaching the end of the race?"

Myra groaned and placed her hands on her hips, leaning forward, her eyes blazing. "Now don't start that again!" she shouted, then lowered her voice, stepping closer as well. "For the last time, I had nothing to do with that man attacking you or the sabotage of your ship!"

"A clever story!" Phineas retorted, his hand gesturing dismissively.

"My ship was sabotaged too!" she replied defensively, crossing her arms. "Or have you forgotten?"

"A red herring!" he insisted, pointing a finger at her.

"A what?" She exclaimed, her face flushing with insult.

"A clever ruse to throw suspicion off yourself!" Phineas insisted, his jaw set stubbornly.

"Now listen here, you old walrus!" she referred to his enormous handlebar mustache. "I've taken just about all I'm going to take from you! Maybe you're the one throwing suspicion off yourself by accusing me!"

Phineas stepped back, gasping, his hand clutching his chest. "Why, you withered-up old prune! Are you accusing me, Professor Phineas B. Hargroves, world-renowned airship captain and inventor, of sabotage?"

"Give me a moment," Myra looked around dramatically, placing her hands on her hips, then continued, "You're the only old walrus in sight!"

Trying to contain his anger, Phineas clenched his fists at his sides. "My dear woman, between the two of us, who has a history of causing destruction?"

Myra's jaw went slack, her eyes widening as if Phineas had crossed a line. "How dare you!" She slapped his face, leaving a red mark. "You were just as responsible for what happened that day as I was!"

Realizing he had gone too far, Phineas immediately softened his expression. "I suppose you're right, and for that, and *only* that, I apologize."

"It's okay," Myra sighed, calming down, her hands dropping to her sides. "I suppose seeing each other again and being this close to returning to the university is making us both on edge."

Phineas nodded, rubbing his cheek where she had slapped him. "The third checkpoint of the race is stationed on campus, right next to the memorial."

"Memorial?" Jedidiah muttered to himself. He was still standing near the top of the ramp, leaning over the rail, listening to their private conversation.

"When was the last time you visited it?" Myra asked, her voice softening.

"It's been at least ten years," Phineas replied, looking down.

"It's only been eight for me," she responded, her eyes distant.

They both stood for a moment in silence, reflecting on a day in their lives nearly twenty years ago. Jedidiah, peeking over the rail of the Swift, wondered with great curiosity what could have happened to turn these two into such bitter rivals. However, his question would not be answered just yet as the two of them turned on their heels and solemnly returned to their ships. In a display of proper sportsmanship, they wished each other good luck as they retired for the night.

****

The next morning, just as dawn broke on Sunday, September 4th, 1881, the air buzzed with anticipation and the promise of adventure. All the contestants began their final preparations, checking their ships and going over last-minute details. The early morning light cast a golden hue over the field, highlighting the sleek forms of the airships.

Mr. Thompson gathered the contestants for a final briefing. "Ladies and gentlemen, the moment we've all been waiting for has arrived. You've faced challenges and shown incredible resilience. Now, it's time to let your skills and ingenuity shine." He pointed to six large chests, each bearing the name of one of the airships. "Each one of you will take one of these trunks with you and deliver it to an official at the first checkpoint. Some are filled with mail, some are filled with supplies ordered by merchants, and some are filled with sandbags."

He handed each contestant an envelope sealed with wax. "You must deliver these envelopes along with the trunks. Don't break the seals or open them. Performing either task will immediately disqualify you. When I fire the starting gun, each of you will race forward, grab a trunk, and take it aboard your vessel. After that, you may embark on the first leg of your journey. May the best airship win!" He aimed the starting gun into the air and fired.

The crowd erupted in cheers, and each contestant sprinted forward to claim their chest. Professor Thaddeus Montgomery, Sir Reginald Fortescue, and Captain Jonathan Braddock assigned their crew members the task of bringing their trunks on board. The hired men, large and muscular with the demeanor of seasoned Navy veterans, effortlessly lifted the hefty cases while the captains hurried to their control panels and initiated their powerful engines.

Phineas B. Hargroves and Tom Miller each grasped one side of the chest associated with the Icarus. They easily hoisted it off the ground and hurried aboard, their expressions filled with determination as they toted the trunk onto the ship.

Jedidiah Davenport and Matthew Colton, however, found lifting their case more challenging. Beads of sweat formed on their foreheads as they struggled, their steps unsteady. "We must have gotten one of the trunks filled with sandbags!" Matthew remarked between panting breaths.

"Must have!" Jedidiah agreed, his breath

coming in short gasps. They exchanged a glance but pressed forward, their muscles straining under the weight.

Myra Wilhelmina Bancroft appeared more prepared than the others. She had brought along a small wooden cart with a miniature steam engine attached. With a confident smile, she lowered a ramp from it, attached a cable to the trunk's handle, and the engine smoothly pulled it up onto the cart. Guiding it aboard the Enigma with a pivoting handle, Myra watched it ascend, satisfaction gleaming in her eyes.

As each team secured their trunks, engines roared to life, and the airships began to lift off one by one. The crowd's cheers grew louder with excitement. The race had officially begun.

As the Swift ascended into the sky, Jedidiah and Matthew finally caught their breath, their earlier struggle now a distant memory. The engines purred steadily, and the landscape below began to shrink, turning into a patchwork of greens and browns.

Jedidiah adjusted a few controls, his focus on the horizon. "We're off to a good start," he said, glancing at Matthew, who nodded in agreement, his eyes scanning the skies for any sign of the other airships.

Meanwhile, down in the cargo hold, the lid of their trunk creaked and slowly began to open.

In the cargo hold of the Swift, the trunk
lid creaked and slowly began to open.

CHAPTER XI

Racing to New York

The horizon stretched endlessly before them, a canvas of blue, promising adventure. Engines roared to life, propellers whirred, and the sky filled with the spirit of competition. Jedidiah Davenport and Matthew Colton aboard the Swift, and Phineas B. Hargroves with Tom Miller on the Icarus, each had their eyes set on the distant goal of New York.

The initial ascent was exhilarating. The airships lifted off gracefully, their sleek forms cutting through the sky. Below, the crowd cheered, faces filled with anticipation. Each vessel surged forward, jockeying for position as they began the long journey through the sky.

Matthew and Jedidiah worked together seamlessly. The light-hearted banter between them added to the relaxed atmosphere on the Swift.

"Look at them go," Matthew remarked, watching Myra's Enigma pull ahead. "Her ship is

Each vessel surged forward,
jockeying for position as they began
the long journey through the sky.

incredible."

Jedidiah nodded, his eyes fixed on the horizon. "She's going to be stiff competition, that's for sure. But we're just getting started. Let's enjoy the journey."

The other airships began to diverge, each taking slightly different routes and making bold maneuvers, causing shifts in the lead. With every surge ahead or fall behind, the race grew more exciting and unpredictable.

On the Icarus, Phineas regaled Tom with stories and wisdom about airship travel, his enthusiasm infectious. Tom listened intently, absorbing every detail and reveling in the adventure.

"You know, Tom," Phineas said, adjusting the controls, "there's more to this race than just speed. It's about strategy, endurance, and knowing when to take risks."

Tom nodded eagerly, his eyes wide with excitement. "I'm just glad to be a part of it, Professor."

The relaxed yet determined atmosphere aboard the Icarus contrasted with the intense competition among the other ships. Phineas and Tom cherished the journey, appreciating the beauty below and the thrill of the race.

As the hours passed, the competition intensified. Myra Wilhelmina Bancroft's Enigma took an early lead, her advanced navigation systems finding efficient routes. Her skill and confidence were evident as she expertly maneuvered her airship. Thaddeus Montgomery faced a minor technical glitch shortly after takeoff but quickly resolved it, showcasing his ingenuity and quick thinking.

Captain Jonathan "Jack" Braddock made a daring move, flying close to a storm front to gain an advantage. The risk paid off, propelling his airship ahead and impressing competitors with his bold tactics. Sir Reginald Fortescue maintained a steady pace, relying on his ship's reliability and disciplined execution to gradually gain ground.

Jedidiah and Matthew initially kept pace with the others but settled into a more leisurely rhythm, savoring the journey as much as the race.

"Look at the sky, Matthew," Jedidiah said, leaning against the railing. "This is what it's all about. The freedom, the adventure."

Matthew smiled, adjusting the controls. "Couldn't agree more, Jed. But let's not forget, we have a race to win."

"Yeah, I guess you're right," Jedidiah agreed as he pushed forward on the throttle, increasing their speed.

Below them, the vast expanse of America unfolded into a patchwork of verdant fields, winding rivers, and dense forests. Each mile brought new sights and experiences, reminding them of the immense beauty and diversity of the landscape.

Jedidiah and Matthew took turns at the controls, ensuring that both could rest and enjoy the journey. During his breaks, Jedidiah leaned back, his mind wandering to the mysterious events of the past weeks. He also kept replaying the conversation he had overheard between Phineas B. Hargroves and Myra Wilhelmina Bancroft. What had happened between the two of them twenty years ago? The mention of that mysterious memorial kept plaguing him. Finally, he resigned himself to the fact that his eccentric friend and mentor would tell him in due time.

Meanwhile, on the Icarus, Phineas and Tom also took turns at the helm, sharing stories and laughter as they navigated the skies. Phineas' vast knowledge of airship mechanics and navigation proved invaluable, and Tom's eagerness to learn made him an excellent student.

"You've got a natural talent for this, Tom," Phineas remarked, watching the young man skillfully adjust the controls. "I wouldn't be surprised if you captained your own ship one day."

Tom's eyes lit up with pride. "Thanks, Professor. I always thought one day I'd end up managing the Spoon Fork freight office or one of the other branches, but I gotta say, this feels right."

Phineas nodded, a twinkle in his eye. "There's

something about the open skies, isn't there? It's a freedom you can't find anywhere else."

Tom glanced around the spacious deck of the Icarus, feeling the gentle sway of the airship beneath his feet. "I never realized how beautiful everything looks from up here. It's like seeing the world for the first time."

Phineas smiled, his gaze distant as he recalled his own first experiences with flight. "I felt the same way when I first took to the skies. There's a sense of adventure, of possibility, that's hard to describe. It's like the world is laid out before you, and you can go anywhere, do anything."

Tom leaned on the railing, looking out at the horizon. "Do you ever get tired of it? The constant travel, the unpredictability?"

"Never," Phineas replied without hesitation. "Every journey is different, every flight a new challenge. It keeps me sharp, keeps me curious. And the people you meet along the way, the places you see... it makes it all worthwhile."

Tom nodded thoughtfully. "I can see that. I guess I never really thought about what it would be like to leave Spoon Fork and see the world. But now, being up here, I can't imagine doing anything else."

Phineas placed a reassuring hand on Tom's shoulder. "You have a natural talent for this, and more importantly, you have the right spirit. I have no doubt you'll go far."

Tom's chest swelled with pride. "Thanks, Professor. That means a lot coming from you. I just hope I can live up to your expectations."

"You already are," Phineas said warmly. "Remember, it's not just about the destination, but the journey itself. And with every flight, you'll learn more, and grow more confident. Just keep your eyes open and your heart adventurous."

The two of them stood in silence for a while, the hum of the engines and the vast expanse of sky their constant companions. At that moment, Tom felt a deep sense of belonging and purpose, realizing that his path was now intertwined with the endless possibilities of the skies.

As they sailed further east, the landscape gradually changed. Rolling hills gave way to sprawling plains, and eventually, the distant outline of the Appalachian Mountains came into view. The air grew cooler, and the changing scenery added to the sense of adventure.

As night fell, the sky transformed into a canvas of stars. The airships continued their journey, the gentle hum of the engines providing a comforting rhythm. Jedidiah and Matthew took turns resting, ensuring they were alert and ready for any challenges that might arise.

Phineas and Tom, too, shared the night watch. The bond between mentor and student grew stronger, forging a connection that went beyond the race. Professor Hargroves took the first watch, while Tom settled into the hammock that Phineas had strung up for him in his cabin.

Myra Wilhelmina Bancroft was the only airship captain without a crewmate, so she had no choice but to trust in her navigation system and take periodic catnaps. As they flew through the night, the anticipation of reaching their first checkpoint fueled everyone's spirits.

****

The next morning, the horizon was painted with the soft hues of dawn. The airships glided smoothly, their crews ready for the day's challenges. Despite the friendly banter and shared moments, each team was acutely aware they were in a race.

Aboard the Swift, Jedidiah and Matthew scanned the sky for any sign of the other airships, but none were in sight. This was expected, as each captain had planned a slightly different route to gain an advantage, and the risk of collisions due to poor lighting at night reinforced their need for space.

Matthew checked the navigation instruments. "The others must be scattered out there. Can't see any of them right now."

Jedidiah grinned. "They're out there, thinking the same thing we are. Let's keep our course steady."

"How far do you think we are from New York?" Matthew asked, scanning the horizon.

Jedidiah adjusted the controls, squinting against the morning light. "If I had to guess, another ten to fourteen hours before we arrive."

Meanwhile, aboard the Icarus, Phineas and Tom were in high spirits. Phineas pointed out landmarks and provided navigational tips.

"Tom, always keep an eye on the horizon as well as your instruments," Phineas advised. "The slightest miscalculation could set us off course."

Tom nodded, glancing back and forth between the sky and the controls. "Got it, Professor. I won't let us down."

Phineas smiled, confidence in Tom growing with each passing moment. "I know you won't. You're doing splendidly."

The other competitors were also deep in their respective strategies. Myra, aboard the Enigma, utilized her advanced navigation systems to maintain her lead, while Jack Braddock and Thaddeus Montgomery each relied on their unique tactics to gain an edge. Sir Reginald Fortescue, true to his methodical nature, maintained a steady pace, his focus unwavering.

The journey had been smooth, but the tension of

the race was ever-present. Each team knew the final stretch to New York would be crucial.

Jedidiah and Matthew shared a quick meal, their spirits high. "We're making good time," Jedidiah said, checking the navigation charts. "If we push a little harder. We can make it by early evening."

Matthew nodded with determination. "Agreed. Let's show them what the Swift can do."

Phineas and Tom also prepared for the final leg of their journey. "We've done well, Tom," Phineas said proudly. "Now, let's bring it home."

Tom's eyes gleamed with excitement. "Yahoo!"

As the afternoon wore on, the skyline of New York City began to emerge in the distance. The Icarus and the Swift arrived almost simultaneously from two different directions. Both airships surged forward, their crews driven by the thrill of nearing their first checkpoint. The competition and sense of adventure that had defined their journey so far culminated in a final push toward their goal.

Jedidiah and Phineas each landed their vessels within moments of each other just after eight o'clock that evening. Only one other airship was present—the Enigma. After mooring the two ships, Phineas, Jedidiah, Matthew, and Tom all rendezvoused at the check-in building. Inside, Myra Wilhelmina Bancroft was talking to one of the officials, looking distraught.

"I'm guessing we're the first three to arrive,"

Jedidiah remarked as he approached the eccentric older woman.

"And you would guess wrong," she replied. "I was the first to arrive at four o'clock."

Phineas raised an eyebrow. "Four o'clock? You must have had some tailwind." Under his breath, he muttered, "Or maybe it was just all of that hot air of yours..."

Choosing to ignore that last remark, Myra smiled proudly. "Indeed. Thaddeus arrived at five, dealing with another minor technical glitch, but he handled it well."

"And the others?" Jedidiah asked curiously.

"Jack made his grand entrance at six," Myra continued. "Always the showman."

"Reginald must have been close behind," Phineas speculated.

"He arrived at seven o'clock sharp," Myra confirmed. "Keeping his usual stoic demeanor despite his later arrival."

Jedidiah chuckled. "And here are the two of us, bringing up the rear."

Phineas patted Jedidiah on the back. "Don't worry, this is just the first checkpoint. We're still in the race."

"Say, Ms. Bancroft," Matthew Colton spoke up. "Where are the others?"

Myra sighed. "On their way to Toronto for the next checkpoint."

"They've already left?" Jedidiah seemed shocked over this news. "How long ago?"

"Reginald left an hour ago," she explained. "Jack left two hours ago, and Thaddeus left three hours ago."

"Gosh!" Tom Miller exclaimed. "They've got that big of a head start on us?"

"We better get checked in so we can leave," Jedidiah turned on his heel to approach the race official. He suddenly stopped and glanced back at the eccentric older woman. "Why haven't you left yet if you got here before anyone else?"

Myra sighed, her shoulders slumping slightly. "The Enigma was sabotaged. After checking in, I went down to the Germania Theatre to see a young friend of mine performing, Lotta Crabtree. When I returned, my ship had been vandalized. It's an easy fix but I'm just waiting for the parts to arrive."

Phineas shrugged as he said, "That's unfortunate. However, my dear woman, perhaps you should have kept your mind on the race and this wouldn't have happened."

"Phineas!" Jedidiah stepped between the two rivals and said, "I think we should all keep our minds on the race!" He turned back to the official. "We need to check in and pick up the wooden box that we'll need to collect the falcons in at the other checkpoints."

The official shook his head. "I can't check either

of you in or give you the boxes until you turn in the chests you brought from Wichita."

Jedidiah frowned but nodded. "I completely forgot!" He turned on his heel and raced out the door, with Matthew right behind. "We'll go get it now!"

Phineas and Tom suddenly realized they had forgotten their trunk as well and followed behind.

As they made their way to the Swift, Jedidiah glanced at Matthew. "Something doesn't feel right."

Matthew nodded in agreement. "I think we should stick around long enough to see if Ms. Bancroft needs our help."

"Agreed," Jedidiah replied as they boarded the Swift and headed to the cargo hold. They grabbed each side of the trunk and prepared to strain lifting it like they had before. Much to their surprise, there was so much weight difference they nearly threw it over their heads.

CHAPTER XII

Aerial Assault

Jedidiah stopped his brow furrowing. "Matt, does this seem lighter to you?"

Matthew hefted one side of the chest, his eyes widening in surprise. "It's definitely lighter. What's going on?"

"Someone has tampered with it!"

"Tampered with it?" Matthew Colton was both shocked and confused. "Are you sure?"

"How else do you explain the sudden difference in weight?" Jedidiah Davenport set his end of the trunk down while Matthew did the same.

Matthew jiggled the latch and tried to open it, but it wouldn't budge. "It's still locked!"

"It is?" Jedidiah asked, perplexed. He suddenly reached inside his vest pocket and removed a small envelope with a wax seal on it. He felt along it while pressing with his fingers. "Just as I thought!" He said aloud, then looked at Matthew. "There's a key inside this envelope. I bet it opens the trunk!"

"Quick!" Colton shouted. "Take it out so we can look inside and see if anything is missing."

"I can't," Jedidiah replied as he replaced the envelope inside his pocket. "If I break the seal, it will disqualify me from the race." He thought for a moment and added, "Besides, we don't even know the original contents anyway. We'll just have to take it to the check-in and face the consequences."

Matthew nodded reluctantly. "Well, we might as well get this over with." They lifted the trunk once more, its lightness still unsettling them. They climbed out of the cargo hold and started back.

After returning to the check-in counter, Jedidiah reluctantly handed over the envelope to the official. The man, who appeared to be in his thirties, smoothed out his beard, stood up, and approached the chest. After breaking the seal, he removed the key and unlocked it. It only took him a moment to compare the contents to the list provided inside the envelope. He glanced back at Davenport and announced that everything was accounted for.

Jedidiah and Matthew immediately breathed a sigh of relief and leaned forward to look inside for themselves. The trunk was mostly empty except for a layer of mail at the bottom.

"So everything is in there?" the young airship captain asked.

"Yes," the official replied matter-of-factly as he

returned to the counter. "Some of the envelopes look a little crumpled and dirty, like someone had been stepping on them, but they're all there." After checking Jedidiah's name off the list, he picked up a small stamped wooden box and handed it over.

Jedidiah thanked him, then turned to Myra Wilhelmina Bancroft and asked, "Would you like some help with your repairs?"

The eccentric older woman sighed and thought for a moment. "I wouldn't mind some extra hands, but I wouldn't want to put you any further behind in the race."

"Gosh, Ms. Bancroft," Matthew Colton spoke up. "We don't mind!"

Jedidiah smiled and quickly added, "Under the circumstances, I think it's the most sportsmanlike thing to do. We never know when or who the saboteurs will attack next. Even though we're competitors, we've got to stick together and help each other as much as possible."

"I agree!" Matthew exclaimed as he turned to look at Phineas B. Hargroves. "Don't you, professor?"

All eyes turned towards the eccentric older man. Phineas wiggled his mustache under his nose and thought carefully before he replied, "Yes, I wholeheartedly agree!" He clapped Matthew on the shoulder and added, "You'll have to tell me all about it after the race, my dear boy!" Without saying another word, he turned on his heel to walk away.

"Phineas," Jedidiah called out to his friend and mentor. "Myra saved your life just a few weeks ago," he reminded him.

Phineas stopped in his tracks. Adjusting his composure, he turned back and said, "A joke! A mere jest! Of course, I would be delighted to stay and further my chances of losing this race." He stopped, cleared his throat, and added, "Er… I mean, I would be delighted to stay and help!"

Grateful for everyone's offer to lend a hand, Myra smiled and said, "The parts should be here soon, and with all of us working together, we'll have the repairs done in no time."

Jedidiah looked around at the bustling city beyond the airfield. "While we wait for the parts, why don't we take a tour of the city? Myra, you could show us around."

"Well, I suppose we have time for a brief tour," Ms. Bancroft replied. "It will be almost an hour before the parts arrive." She looked at the eccentric older man and asked, "Will you be joining us?"

Phineas shook his head. "I will stay behind to keep an eye on the airships. The vandals may still be lurking about. The rest of you go ahead and enjoy."

Tom Miller suddenly spoke and offered to stay with Phineas and help guard the airships.

While the crew of the Icarus returned to their post, Jedidiah, Myra, and Matthew ventured into New York City, their eyes wide with wonder. The skyline was dotted with tall buildings, a stark contrast to the open skies they had just traveled through. The streets were bustling with people, horse-drawn carriages, and street vendors.

The trio made their way through the crowded streets, taking in the sights and sounds of the city. The noise and energy were overwhelming yet exhilarating. They passed by newsboys shouting headlines and women in elegant dresses strolling down the sidewalks.

"This place is incredible," Matthew said, his eyes darting from one building to the next. "I've never seen anything like it. It's even bigger than Wichita!"

"It's certainly got Spoon Fork beat," Jedidiah added, his eyes shining with curiosity. "The architecture is stunning. Look at that building over there!"

As they strolled through the bustling streets of New York, Myra pointed out various landmarks. "That beautiful apartment building overlooks Central Park. It hasn't been officially named yet, but rumors have it that it's going to be called the Dakota. And over there is Central Park itself, an oasis in the middle of all this chaos."

Myra next led them to a quaint café near the

park. "This is one of my favorite spots," she said, gesturing to a small table outside. "Perfect for a quick rest and a cup of coffee."

They sat down, enjoying the ambiance of the busy street. Jedidiah took a sip of his coffee, savoring the rich flavor. "This is fantastic. I can see why you like it here, Myra."

Myra smiled, looking around the bustling city. "New York has a charm of its own. It's chaotic, but there's a certain beauty in its energy and diversity."

They spent the next forty-five minutes exploring the city's iconic locations, starting with the grandeur of St. Patrick's Cathedral and then moving on to see where they had begun construction on Union Square.

As they continued their stroll, Jedidiah's attention was suddenly caught by a glint in a shop window. He paused, peering through the glass at a beautifully ornate pocket watch displayed prominently. Its intricate brass casing featured delicate filigree work surrounding a green gem in the center. The craftsmanship was exquisite, drawing Jedidiah in with its elegance and mystery.

"I'll catch up with the two of you in a moment," Jedidiah said, his eyes still fixed on the watch. "I want to take a closer look at something."

Matthew and Myra nodded, continuing their exploration while Jedidiah entered the quaint shop. The interior was dimly lit, filled with curiosities and antiques from various eras. Behind the counter stood a woman in plain attire, her demeanor calm and composed. On the wall behind her hung a sign depicting an octopus wearing a top hat and monocle.

"Good afternoon," Jedidiah greeted, approaching the counter. "I couldn't help but notice the pocket watch in your window. It's quite remarkable."

The shop owner, a middle-aged woman with strikingly sharp eyes, glanced at the watch and then back at Jedidiah. "Ah, yes," she said with a knowing smile. "It is indeed a special piece."

Jedidiah leaned closer, admiring the detailed work. "Is it for sale?"

She shook her head slowly. "I'm afraid not. It's one of a kind and priceless. It's not time for me to part with it yet."

Her words intrigued Jedidiah. There was something almost cryptic about her response, but he didn't press further. "I understand. It's truly a masterpiece."

As he turned to leave, a newspaper on the counter caught his eye. The headline read: "Important Artifact Stolen from the British Museum in London." He skimmed the article, noting that the stolen item was of significant historical value and its theft had caused an international stir.

The shop owner noticed his interest and said, "Terrible news, isn't it? The world seems to be full of mysteries and adventures these days."

Jedidiah nodded, a thoughtful expression on his face. "Indeed, it is. Anyway, I have to go now. Thank you for letting me admire the watch. Perhaps our paths will cross again."

"I believe they will," she replied, her eyes twinkling with a hint of foresight. "Safe travels, Mr. Davenport."

Jedidiah left the shop, rejoining Matthew and Myra with the image of the watch and the mysterious shop owner lingering in his mind.

Back at the airfield, Phineas and Tom kept a watchful eye on all three airships. "Do you think they're having a good time?" Tom asked, peering towards the city.

"I'm sure they are," Phineas replied, his eyes scanning the horizon. "You could have gone with them, you know."

"I know, but I made a commitment to help safeguard these vessels, and I mean to see it through," the young man replied. "We still have a long way to go."

Phineas wholeheartedly agreed.

Just after nine o'clock, Jedidiah, Myra, and Matthew returned to the airfield, their spirits lifted by their brief adventure. The parts for Myra's airship had arrived, and Phineas and Tom had already started the repairs.

"How was the city?" Phineas asked, wiping his hands.

"Incredible," Jedidiah replied, a wide grin on his face. "I definitely want to come back here when we have more time to spend."

"Good to hear," Phineas said. "Now, let's get this ship fixed and back in the race."

The group worked together for the next two hours making the repairs. Once they were finished, the Enigma was as good as new and ready to set sail.

Myra Wilhelmina Bancroft properly thanked everyone, and each set of workers returned to their respective ships. The engines of the Swift, Icarus, and Enigma roared to life as they lifted off from New York, slicing through the cool night air. The sky was a canvas of stars, with the three airships casting shadows over the city below. They had a long journey ahead, and the crews settled in for a night of steady flying.

Aboard the Swift, Jedidiah and Matthew took turns at the controls, their eyes scanning the horizon for any sign of trouble. The night was calm, and the airship hummed along at a consistent pace.

"How long do you think it'll take us to reach Toronto?" Matthew asked, adjusting the throttle slightly

"At our current speed, we should get there between ten am and noon," Jedidiah replied.

"You think we still have a chance?" Matthew asked reluctantly.

"Well, we have half of the racers right here," Jedidiah chuckled, banking the ship slightly. "Anything is possible."

****

As the hours ticked by, the three airships made good progress. They passed over small towns and vast stretches of wilderness, the landscape bathed in the soft glow of the moon. The crews remained alert, knowing that the race was far from over.

On the Icarus, Phineas and Tom engaged in lively conversation.

"Remember, Tom," Phineas said, pointing to a cluster of stars, "those constellations can help you find your way when all else fails. Always trust your instincts and the stars."

Tom nodded, absorbing every word. "I understand, Professor. I'll keep that in mind." He involuntarily yawned and stretched as he said it.

Phineas smiled and instructed his young friend to lie down in his hammock and take a nap. He assured Tom he could handle it alone.

Meanwhile, on the Enigma, Myra meticulously monitored her advanced navigation systems, ensuring she was on the most efficient path. She glanced out at the other airships, her mind focused on maintaining her slight lead. At one point, she considered lying down and taking a nap but didn't want to risk it.

The Swift hummed along steadily, with Jedidiah and Matthew taking turns at the controls. The serene night offered a sense of peace, but both men remained vigilant.

"I wonder how much of a lead the others have on us," Matthew mused, adjusting the throttle slightly.

"Not as much as they'd like to think," Jedidiah replied confidently. "We've made up a lot of time, and with any luck, we'll catch up with them in Toronto."

****

Around 3 AM, the skies began to darken ominously. The previously clear night gave way to heavy clouds, and the wind picked up, buffeting the airships.

Matthew, still taking his turn at the helm, tightened his grip on the controls. "Looks like a storm is coming," he said to himself. "I need to wake Jed up!"

Lightning flashed across the sky, illuminating the dark clouds in stark relief. Thunder rumbled in the distance, growing louder with each passing minute.

During one of the lurches of the ship, Tom Miller, who had been sound asleep rocking back and forth in his hammock, was suddenly thrown to the floor. It took him a moment to realize where he was, and he immediately raced out onto the deck of the Icarus. "What happened?" he asked. "Is everything okay?"

"Everything is fine," Phineas replied, not taking his hands off the wheel. "Keep your eyes on the instruments," he instructed. "This storm could get rough."

The three airships battled the elements, their frames creaking under the strain of the turbulent winds. Rain lashed against the sides of the cabins and blew sideways onto the decks. Visibility dropped dramatically. This went on for the next three hours until it finally subsided.

As dawn began to break, painting the sky with hues of pink and orange, the storm was finally over. The airships emerged from the clouds, battered but fortunately not bruised. They were still flying high.

Later in the day, as they were crossing over the border into Canada, they found themselves flying over the expansive waters of Lake Ontario. The vast lake stretched out beneath them, its surface glistening in the sunlight and creating a dazzling display of light and shadow. From their vantage point in the sky, they could see the gentle waves rolling across the water, the deep blue contrasting with the green of the surrounding shoreline. Small boats dotted the lake, appearing as tiny specks moving leisurely across the vast expanse. The sight was breathtaking, a testament to the natural beauty of the region.

As they drew closer to their checkpoint in Toronto, the thrill of the journey and the anticipation of the race filled the air, making the scene even more exhilarating.

Suddenly, the calm was shattered by an unknown airship appearing on the horizon. It was unlike any they had seen before, with sleek, dark lines and an aura of menace.

Jedidiah spotted it first. "Look at that!"

"Gosh!" Matthew Colton exclaimed. "Who is it?"

"It's none of the other contestants," Jedidiah replied. "That's for sure!"

"What's it doing here?" Matthew removed the goggles from the brim of his hat, placed them over his eyes, and said, "It's coming this way."

Before anyone could react, the unknown airship closed the distance rapidly. A low hum resonated through the air, growing louder by the second.

Without warning, a beam of energy shot from the unknown airship, striking the Enigma.

"What's happening to Ms. Bancroft's ship?"

Matthew shouted. "It's rocking back and forth like it's riding on waves!" Before Jedidiah could respond, the Enigma suddenly began to descend toward the ground.

Suddenly, the same beam that struck the Enigma was turned toward the Swift. A wave of nausea overcame both Jedidiah Davenport and Matthew Colton. The young men began staggering across the deck, trying to keep from falling. The Swift rocked violently from side to side as Jedidiah clung to the wheel.

"We're going to have to land!" he shouted.

"Land!" Matthew replied, gripping the rail and hanging his head over the side, violently ill. "I don't care what you have to do, just make this stop!"

As they began their descent, Phineas frantically worked the controls of the Icarus, trying to outmaneuver whoever was attacking them, his face set in grim determination.

"What's going on, Professor Hargroves?" Tom Miller asked frantically. "I didn't hear any gunfire. Why are they going down?"

"I don't know, but I'm going to find out," Phineas motioned for his young apprentice to come closer. "Take hold of the wheel!" he shouted.

The eccentric older man, now with both hands free, placed his telescopic goggles over his eyes, ran toward the railing, and trained his eyes on the unknown attacker. Through the magnified lenses, he saw a menacing device protruding from the side of the airship. It was a massive contraption, intricately designed with brass gears, copper tubing, and an ominous-looking horn-shaped muzzle that seemed to vibrate with a low, sinister hum. Pulsating with energy, the cannon's intricate mechanisms, and finely tuned dials indicated a level of precision engineering that was both awe-inspiring and terrifying.

"My word!" he exclaimed in terror. "It's an ultrasonic disruptor cannon!"

"A what?" Tom asked, confused.

"You're about to find out!"

The ultrasonic disruptor cannon, with its intricate gears and brass fittings, unleashed a wave of chaos aimed directly at them. The Icarus shuddered violently. Phineas and Tom began to stagger just like Jedidiah and Matthew had. The eccentric older man tried in vain to stumble back to the helm but was forced to rush back to the rail, becoming violently ill like Matthew a few minutes earlier.

"You're going to have to land this ship!" he shouted to his apprentice.

"Me?" Tom replied in shock, trying not to drop to his knees. "I've never landed an airship before!"

"My dear boy," Phineas raised his head and said, "there's a first time for everything!" He quickly hung his head back over the railing. After a moment, he looked up and said, "Just do as I say!"

Following Phineas' exact instructions, Tom began to guide the Icarus towards the ground, along with the others. With a final jolt, it landed roughly in a field a few hundred yards away from the Swift and the Enigma, its frame creaking and groaning. The impact sent up clouds of dust and debris but miraculously sustained no serious damage.

Jedidiah and Matthew were the first to emerge from their ship, followed by Myra, then quickly joined by Phineas and Tom. All still reeling from the aftermath of the attack, they stood in the field, staring up at the unknown airship that hovered menacingly above them.

The attacking vessel floated down close enough for everyone to see who was assaulting them. A mysterious figure dressed in all black, wearing a peaked cap that sat ominously atop his plague mask, looked down at them. Even though they couldn't see his face, they could sense his pleasure in what he had just accomplished. With one last act of defiance, he leaned over the rail and dropped a round metal object directly above them. Before anyone could react, the item hit the ground, and smoke began to fill the air. Each of them collapsed almost immediately, losing consciousness. Phineas glanced up just before passing out and spotted the assailant removing his mask. Phineas' last words were, "It can't be you!"

The mysterious figure leaned over the
rail and dropped a round metal object
from directly above them.

CHAPTER XIII

Rescue Plans

The warm morning sun shone brightly as Jedidiah, Matthew, and Tom regained consciousness, groggy and disoriented from the sudden attack. However, judging by the sun's position, not much time had passed. As they shook off the last remnants of unconsciousness, a sense of urgency gripped them.

Jedidiah glanced around to ensure everyone was okay. He spotted Matthew and Tom but noticed Phineas and Myra were missing. "Phincas? Myra?" Jedidiah called out, his voice hoarse.

"They're gone," Matthew said, his voice filled with alarm. "Whoever attacked us took them."

"Gone?" Tom stood up, rubbing his head, his expression worried. "We need to find them, fast."

"How long were we out this time?" Matthew asked, concerned.

Jedidiah glanced at his watch and replied, "Less

than an hour."

"At least it wasn't three like last time," Matthew muttered, trying to look on the bright side.

Taking a deep breath to calm his racing heart, Jedidiah suggested, "Let's inspect the airships first. We've got to make sure they didn't get hurt during the landings. We can use them to search for Phineas and Myra."

After a quick inspection of the Icarus and the Enigma, finding no serious damage, they headed towards the Swift. As they approached, they heard a faint noise coming from the cargo hold. Exchanging knowing glances, they cautiously approached.

Jedidiah opened the hatch and saw movement under a tarp. He lifted it, revealing a young man with a nervous look on his face.

"Who are you?" Jedidiah demanded, his tone firm.

The young man hesitated, then attempted to make a run for it. Tom Miller, anticipating this move, tackled him to the ground. Jedidiah and Matthew swiftly joined in, helping Tom restrain the young man, who raised his hands in surrender.

"This is the one I told you about!" Tom exclaimed excitedly, his eyes widening with recognition. He pointed an accusatory finger at the young man. "He's the one who hit me over the head and sabotaged both the Icarus and the Phoenix."

Jedidiah stepped forward, his face tightening with anger. He leaned in closer to the young man, his eyes blazing. "So you're the one who's been vandalizing all the airships in the race!"

"No!" the young man protested, his hands trembling. "I had nothing to do with that."

"Don't lie!" Tom shouted, his voice cracking with fury. He tried to step between Jedidiah and the stranger, but Matthew placed his hands firmly on Tom's shoulders and pulled him back, saying, "Easy, Tom. We'll handle this."

Tom took a deep breath, his eyes still blazing with anger. "You did something to Professor Hargroves' and Mr. Davenport's ships after you knocked me out!" he continued to accuse the stranger.

"Listen, kid," the young man replied, his voice edged with desperation. "I never knocked you out, and I admit I was planning to sabotage both the Phoenix and the Icarus, but those other two beat me to it. They were the ones who knocked you out, not me!"

"You can go peddle your fish somewhere else because I ain't buying it!" Tom retorted, his face flushed with anger. "And stop calling me 'kid'! I'm eighteen years old. How old are you?"

"Twenty," the stranger replied smugly, lifting his chin defiantly.

"Big man," Tom scoffed, stepping forward

aggressively, his fists clenched. "And you did knock me out!"

"You were hit from behind, remember!" the young man shot back, his voice rising with frustration.

"So?"

"You were facing me when it happened!" the young man exploded, throwing his hands up in exasperation. "How could I have hit you from behind?"

"Oh yeah," Tom muttered, his anger deflating as he remembered that detail. He looked down, feeling a bit foolish. "But you sabotaged those ships, and you've been vandalizing all the others as well!"

"I swear I had nothing to do with those attacks!" the young man said earnestly.

"Why should we believe you?" Matthew asked, narrowing his eyes suspiciously. "Who are you anyway?"

"My name is Edwin, and I'm telling the truth," he replied firmly. "Yes, I was going to do it, but I never did."

"I'm sure you had something to do with Professor Hargroves and Ms. Bancroft being kidnapped too!" Tom shouted, stepping forward again, his face flushed with accusation.

"Aunt Myra's been kidnapped?" Edwin echoed, his eyes widening with genuine shock.

"Yes, Aunt Myra has been..." Tom cut his sentence short and, with a look of shock, asked, "Ms. Bancroft is your aunt?"

"Yes," Edwin nodded earnestly. "Myra Wilhelmina Bancroft is my aunt."

Jedidiah held up a hand, gesturing for Tom to calm down. "I'll take it from here." He studied Edwin's face, sensing a mix of fear and determination. "How did you get aboard the Swift?"

Edwin hesitated, then sighed. "I was hiding in the trunk you picked up in Wichita and delivered to New York."

Matthew's eyes widened in realization. "That's why the trunk was so much lighter when we dropped it off at the checkpoint!" He furrowed his brow. "But the trunk was locked. I checked it myself, and the key was sealed in an envelope. How did you get in and out?"

"I picked the lock to get in and again from the inside to get out," Edwin shrugged.

Jedidiah pondered this for a moment and asked, "So, Myra really is your aunt, and you had nothing to do with the vandalism?"

"On my word!" Edwin Bancroft swore, looking Jedidiah directly in the eyes. "I would never do anything to endanger Aunt Myra."

Jedidiah's expression softened slightly. He pulled out a folded piece of paper from his hip pocket. "Did you drop this the night of the party after the Founder's Day celebration at my ranch?"

Edwin's eyes widened with fear. "I... I don't know. Let me see it."

Jedidiah unfolded the paper and handed it to Edwin. He examined the logo and the handwritten numbers. A wave of relief washed over his face. "I've never seen this before," he said, shaking his head. "I swear."

Jedidiah studied Edwin's face and saw sincerity there. "If you're telling the truth, we could use your help. Do you have any idea who would have taken Phineas and Myra?"

Edwin shook his head, his expression troubled. "The man who forced me into this—he's dangerous and has been orchestrating all of this from the shadows. But I don't know where his hideout is. He's always contacted me. But I'm pretty sure it's somewhere close by. He's mentioned his connections in Toronto."

"You were forced into it?" Jedidiah asked curiously, raising an eyebrow.

"Yes," Edwin admitted, looking down with a sigh, not proud of his next words. "I had a lot of gambling debt, and this man paid it off, but in exchange, he made me agree to do things for him. One of which was to sabotage your airships. He said he had some heavy bets placed on the outcome and wanted to guarantee that my Aunt Myra would be the winner."

"Then why was Myra's ship vandalized along with the others?" Jedidiah asked, puzzled, trying to figure out if Edwin was telling the truth.

"I don't know," Edwin admitted, shaking his head. "Unless there's someone else with their own pick for the winner." He looked pleadingly at Jedidiah. "Please believe me!"

Jedidiah thought it over for a moment and decided to take the young man's word, at least for now. "Okay, we need to figure out where they've been taken and form a rescue plan. If it was the person you've been working for, we can start by looking around here."

"*If* it was?" Matthew spoke up, his brow furrowed. "Sounds like it *definitely* was to me."

"Something doesn't make sense," Jedidiah replied, rubbing his chin thoughtfully. "Why would this person claim to want to make Myra the winner and then kidnap her?"

"So you think there is a third party out there?" Matthew asked, looking perplexed.

"I don't know," Jedidiah admitted, shaking his head. "Either way, we can't just keep standing here."

"What are we gonna do if they use that ultrasonic disrupter cannon on us again?" Tom asked, his voice filled with concern.

"Ultrasonic disrupter cannon?" Jedidiah and

Matthew said in unison, their faces showing a mix of confusion and realization.

"That's what Professor Hargroves called the weapon that was used against us," Tom Miller explained, his eyes wide with worry.

Edwin's face lit up with a glimmer of hope. "I think I know a way! There's a place in Toronto called Automaton Alley. They would have the parts and blueprints we need to build our own."

"Your employer dealt with these people?" Jedidiah asked, inquiring.

"Yes and no," Edwin replied mysteriously. "Yes, he dealt with them, but no, they're not exactly... people."

Jedidiah eyed the young man suspiciously. "I want you to take me to this place. We'll go in the Swift." Turning towards Matthew and Tom, he said, "The two of you take the Icarus and search the area. Find out where we are and see if any of the locals have seen anything."

Matthew and Tom nodded, their determination mirrored in their eyes. "Be careful," Matthew said, his voice filled with concern.

"You too," Jedidiah replied, giving them a reassuring nod. "Let's do this for Phineas and Myra."

Jedidiah and Edwin boarded the Swift, its engines roaring to life as they lifted off toward Toronto. Matthew and Tom watched as the airship disappeared into the distance, then turned and boarded the Icarus. Matthew was a bit nervous about flying solo. He had become quite the pilot in the months following the incident with the D.&R.W. Railroad, but this would be his first time completely on his own. He tried to hide his concerns from Tom as he started the engine, taking a deep breath as the ship began to leave the ground.

Matthew and Tom scoured the area from above for quite some time, occasionally descending to ask locals if they had seen anything unusual. The answer was always no. Finally, they spotted a small child playing in a field. They hovered close enough to ask him if he had seen an airship flying over that morning.

"I have indeed, sir," the small boy replied. "Yours is the second one."

"When did you see the first one?" Matthew asked quickly.

"Over an hour ago," he pointed towards the harbor. "It flew over the warehouses over there and then dipped out of sight."

Matthew glanced at Tom. "Sounds like that's where they landed!" Turning back to the small boy, he said, "Thank you. You've helped more than you could know!"

"Any time, mister!" the boy replied.

"What's your name, kid?" Tom asked, feeling a sense of pleasure in using the term on someone else.

"Albert, sir," he replied. "Albert Wilson Jackson. My family owns a store here in Port Whitby."

"Whitby!" Matthew exclaimed. "So that's the town we're in, Whitby, Ontario!" With this crucial information, they knew where to direct their efforts.

Back in the Swift, Jedidiah and Edwin quickly made their way toward Toronto. The city sprawled before them, a bustling metropolis with its spires and towers gleaming in the afternoon sun. Edwin stood nervously on the deck, occasionally glancing over the side as if expecting trouble.

"You're sure this place in Automaton Alley will have what we need?" Jedidiah asked, breaking the silence.

"Yes," Edwin replied confidently. "They specialize in all sorts of mechanical parts and contraptions. If anyone has the components to build a countermeasure against that disrupter cannon, it's them."

Jedidiah nodded thoughtfully. "And you're certain you can trust them?"

Edwin hesitated for a moment before answering. "As much as anyone can trust someone in this business. They're not exactly law-abiding citizens, but they have a reputation for keeping their deals and their secrets."

"Good enough for me," Jedidiah said with a hint of a smile. "We'll need to move quickly once we get there. Every minute counts."

As the Swift descended toward Toronto, both men braced themselves for what lay ahead. The urgency of their mission weighed heavily on their minds, knowing that Phineas and Myra's lives depended on their next moves.

They landed the Swift on some farmland just outside the city, navigated their way through the streets, and turned down the narrow lane known as Automaton Alley. The street was a hive of activity, filled with stores selling mechanical parts, inventive contraptions, and everything in between.

They spotted a shop specializing in weaponry. Standing in front of the entrance was a large mechanical man made of gears and cogs, covered in a shiny brass casing. He wore a top hat with goggles resting on the brim and a vest adorned with intricate designs. His eyes looked like a second set of goggles attached directly to his face, giving him an intense and focused expression. The mechanical man also had a prominent bow tie and various mechanical components visible on his chest.

"That's a very interesting display," Jedidiah remarked as he studied the mechanical man. "It almost looks like it could talk to me!"

"Uh, Mr. Davenport," Edwin tried to speak up.

"Call me Jed."

Standing in front of the entrance was a large
mechanical man made of gears and cogs.

"Okay, Jed..."

"Look, it can wait. Let's go inside and find the owner of the shop." Jedidiah waved off the young man as he turned to march inside the building. Suddenly, the mechanical man's arm moved and blocked his entrance. Davenport was obviously taken aback by this. He looked up at the machine's face and almost fainted as it looked back at him.

"The hu...man who owns the shop and my...self is not here to...day," the mechanical man announced. His face was devoid of expression, and his mouth did not move. His voice seemed to come from some type of speaker below the part of his face where his nose should have been. The words were accompanied by slight pauses and mechanical stutters, attempting to add to the eerie lifelike quality of his speech. "Per...haps, I can be of as...sistance to you."

Jedidiah just stood there, blinking his eyes rapidly as he was now at a total loss for words.

****

Back in Whitby, Matthew and Tom had already begun flying over the warehouses in search of Phineas B. Hargroves and Myra Wilhelmina Bancroft.

"Keep your eyes peeled," Matthew instructed, adjusting the controls for a smoother glide. "There has to be something here."

Tom nodded, his eyes darting between the buildings and the ground below. "Do you think we'll spot them?"

"I hope so," Matthew replied. "But we have to be careful. We don't know who we're dealing with yet."

As they flew over the last row of warehouses, Tom spotted something unusual. "There!" he shouted, pointing toward a large building near the water. "Do you see that?"

Matthew slipped on his goggles while his gaze followed Tom's finger. A large, ominous airship, partially concealed by the building's shadow, was docked next to the warehouse.

"That's it," Matthew confirmed, his grip tightening on the controls. "We found it."

Tom's excitement was tempered by a sense of caution. "Should we wait for Jedidiah and what's his name to come back, or do we attempt to rescue them alone?"

"We wait," Matthew decided. "We can't risk engaging them by ourselves. We need to be smart about this."

They circled the area, keeping a safe distance while maintaining visual contact with the airship. The minutes ticked by slowly, each one filled with tension and anticipation.

As they waited, Tom suddenly gasped.

"Matthew, look!"

A group of figures emerged from the warehouse, heading toward the airship. Among them were Phineas and Myra, their hands bound and guarded by armed men. The leader still concealed his identity with a plague mask.

"We can't just sit here!" Tom exclaimed, his fists clenching in frustration.

"I know," Matthew said, his jaw set with determination. "But we have to stick to the plan. Jedidiah will be here soon."

Tom, frustration evident on his face, took a deep breath. "We need to buy some time. If we can delay their takeoff, we might stand a chance."

Matthew nodded, guiding the Icarus down toward a secluded spot behind a cluster of warehouses. They landed smoothly, hidden from view. "Let's move quickly and quietly," he whispered as they disembarked.

The two crept through the shadows, keeping low and out of sight. They maneuvered around crates and machinery, making their way toward the enemy airship. As they approached, they could hear the guards talking, their voices gruff and impatient.

Tom spotted a stack of barrels near the airship. "If we can create a distraction," he suggested, "maybe we can delay them long enough for Mr. Davenport to get here."

Matthew nodded, his mind racing. "Alright. I'll

sneak around to the other side and see if I can find a way to board the ship. You create the distraction."

Tom gave a quick nod and moved toward the barrels, positioning himself carefully. He found a loose piece of metal and struck it against a stone, creating a loud clanging noise. The guards immediately turned their attention to the sound, weapons at the ready.

"What was that?" one of the guards barked, gesturing for a couple of others to investigate.

As they moved towards Tom, Matthew took the opportunity to slip inside the airship. He located the engine compartment, where he began working quickly to disable it. He pulled a few pipes loose just enough to make it look like they had vibrated apart. He tampered with other parts of the ship's steam-powered engine, just enough to delay their departure. Matthew didn't want to tip their hand too early.

Tom, meanwhile, continued to make noise, keeping the guards occupied. He threw small rocks and debris to different spots, making it seem like there were more people sneaking around.

Finally, Matthew rejoined Tom, and they retreated a safe distance to observe the results of their handiwork. The guards, confused and on high alert, returned to the airship, only to discover from their masked leader that the engines were malfunctioning. Shouts of frustration and anger filled the air as they scrambled to fix the problem.

Phineas and Myra, still bound, looked around anxiously. Phineas caught sight of Matthew and Tom hiding behind some crates and managed a subtle nod of acknowledgment.

"We did it," Tom whispered a hint of relief in his voice. "Now we just need to hold out until Jedidiah and Edwin arrive."

Just then, a thought struck Tom, and he turned to Matthew. "How will Mr. Davenport know how to find us?"

"Well, he'll just..." Matthew cut his sentence short as realization suddenly dawned on him. "Here's the new plan. You're going to stay here and keep an eye on everything while I fly the Icarus to Toronto and hopefully intercept Jed as he's heading back."

Tom grabbed Matthew's arm as another thought occurred to him. "What if he's already on his way to where we left the Enigma?"

Matthew rethought his plan and came up with a new idea. "Okay, so instead of flying straight to Toronto, I'll head to that field first. After that, I'll plot an intercept course for the city."

Still crouching to avoid detection, Matthew Colton looked back one last time to make sure Tom wasn't going to say anything else. When he saw that the young man was remaining silent, Matthew smiled and said, "Just stay low and keep out of sight. We're counting on you."

Feeling a genuine sense of pride from being trusted with such an important assignment, Tom saluted his superior and said, "You can count on me, boss!"

"Now cut that out!" Matthew laughed as he turned and cautiously started making his way back to the airship. "I won't be long!"

As Tom Miller watched the Icarus flying away, he was completely unaware of a strange man sneaking up behind him. He turned just in time to see him swinging a wooden axe handle directly at his head!

CHAPTER XIV

Automaton Alley

Unaware of the danger unfolding near the warehouse in Whitby, Jedidiah stood speechless, staring at the mechanical man who had just spoken to him. The shiny brass casing and top hat gave the automaton an almost whimsical appearance, but its movements and unblinking eyes were anything but playful.

"Per...haps, I can be of as...sistance to you," the machine repeated, its voice emanating from a hidden speaker, its words continuing to be broken by slight pauses and mechanical stutters.

Edwin, noticing Jedidiah's stunned expression, stepped forward cautiously. "We're looking for parts and blueprints."

"Fol...low me," the automaton said, its voice mechanical yet clear. It turned with precise, jerky movements, gears whirring softly as it walked inside the shop. Its steps were deliberate, each joint moving with the calculated efficiency of well-oiled machinery.

Before entering the building, Davenport turned to Edwin and asked, "Why didn't you tell me this thing could talk?"

"I kind of figured you knew," Edwin replied innocently. "After all, the name of this street is Automaton Alley..." He waited for Jedidiah's response, but Davenport continued staring blankly at him. "You do know what an automaton is, don't you?"

The young entrepreneur felt a twinge of offense at the question. After all, he was regarded as a skilled engineer with several inventions under his belt.

"Of course I know what an automaton is!" He quickly scanned their surroundings to ensure no one was eavesdropping before continuing, "But just to make sure we're on the same page, why don't you tell me what your understanding of one is?"

Edwin chuckled softly. "An automaton is a self-operating machine, often designed to resemble and mimic human actions. In our world of steam and gears, these intricate devices use complex mechanical systems. They can perform a variety of tasks with an eerie, lifelike precision. Here in Automaton Alley, they're quite common and serve various purposes, from labor to security. Some are even designed for interaction, like our friend here."

Jedidiah nodded thoughtfully, absorbing Edwin's explanation. "Alright, that makes sense. Let's go inside and see what we can find." But before he took a single step, he looked back at the younger man as something dawned on him. "Why did it sound like you were reading that off something?"

Edwin smiled and glanced over at a plaque hanging on the wall next to Jedidiah. Everything he had just said was written on it.

Davenport merely rolled his eyes and shook his head. "Let's go in!" He turned and stepped down from the wooden sidewalk into the shop.

Once inside, Jedidiah's gaze quickly darted between the automaton and the array of mechanical wonders displayed in the storefront windows. Edwin walked beside him, his eyes scanning the workshop for any signs of danger.

The vast interior of the building was a labyrinth of shelves filled with gears, cogs, and various mechanical contraptions. There were parts strewn across workbenches, some in various stages of assembly, and others meticulously arranged in labeled drawers.

As they moved further into the shop, Jedidiah's eyes widened in surprise. Standing in the corner, almost hidden behind a shelf of gears and cogs, was a second mechanical man. This one was nearly identical to the first but had slight differences in its construction and its eyes had a softer glow.

"Look at that," Jedidiah whispered, nudging Edwin. "There's another one."

Edwin glanced over, not as surprised as Jedidiah but still impressed. "They don't call this Automaton Alley for nothing," he murmured, a mix of awe and apprehension in his voice.

The second automaton remained motionless, its presence adding to the eerie atmosphere of the shop. Jedidiah couldn't help but feel a sense of unease as they followed the first automaton further into the labyrinthine interior, its precise, jerky movements echoing in the dimly lit space.

The mechanical man paused and turned to face the second one. Its eyes brightened and dimmed in a rhythmic pattern, resembling Morse code. The second automaton responded in the same way, its eyes flickering in a similar pattern. Jedidiah watched the exchange, his brow furrowing in curiosity.

"They're talking to each other," he deduced. "They have their own language!"

Edwin nodded. "Some automatons aren't equipped to communicate vocally," he explained. "They're strictly service machines, designed for specific tasks. This light signaling must be their way of conveying information to each other."

At this moment, the first mechanical man motioned for them to follow him to an oak desk at the back of the shop, while the second one picked up a large crate filled with blueprints and a few intricate devices and brought it to them.

"So there's no one else I can speak with?" Jedidiah glanced up from the crate, his brow furrowed in frustration.

"There is on...ly one hu...man associated with this shop and he is not here to...day," the mechanical man explained.

Jedidiah stepped forward, his resolve returning. "We need parts and blueprints for an ultrasonic disruptor cannon. We don't have much time," he said urgently.

"That's a ve...ry specific and pow...erful piece of equip...ment," the machine replied.

"I realize that," Jedidiah said, growing impatient. His fingers drummed on the crate as he spoke. "Do you have what I need or not?"

"A similar weapon is being used against us," Edwin spoke up, his eyes darting between Jedidiah and the automaton. "We need to build our own to counter it and rescue our friends."

The mechanical man's glowing eyes brightened and dimmed alternately as it processed the information given. Finally, it replied, "The blue...prints are in the crate." Without saying another word, it turned and walked through two double doors leading into a storage room.

"Thank you," Jedidiah said sarcastically, rolling

The second mechanical man picked up a
large crate filled with blueprints and a few
intricate devices and brought it to them.

his eyes as the machine vanished from sight. He began to browse through the trunk, his fingers trembling with a mix of anger and disbelief. His eyes widened in shock as he recognized several of the designs. There were duplicates of the plans for every one of his airships: The Phoenix, The Navigator, The Eclipse, and The Drifter. He even found a copy of the blueprints for his high-powered scope and range finder for his rifle.

"This is... outrageous," Jedidiah muttered, clenching his fists. "These are my designs. How did they get here?" He spotted a copy of the original blueprint for the Icarus that he received from Phineas. His automatic telegraph designs, the small generator for operating the roofs of his hangars. As he dug deeper, he found the blueprints for the cannon and various other weapons that were unfamiliar to him. "Every one of these designs has been stolen!" he exclaimed, his voice rising with anger.

Edwin glanced over, his eyes widening in disbelief. "Stolen? How could someone have gotten hold of the blueprints to your airships, and other inventions like your telegraph or scope..."

Jedidiah suddenly whirled around from the crate and grabbed the younger man by the collar, his eyes blazing with fury. "I never said out loud what designs were in there. How did you know what was inside?" he demanded, shaking Edwin slightly.

Edwin took a deep breath, knowing he had no choice but to come clean. He began to recount the events of that fateful night, his voice trembling as he relived the memory. It was over two weeks ago, but he could still remember every detail.

****

It all happened the night you caught me in the hangar. I remember it vividly—sneaking onto the ranch, every rustle of leaves threatening to expose me. The moon hung high, casting long, dancing shadows in the wind. I stayed to the edges, creeping along, desperate to remain unseen. The man who'd ensnared me was clear: retrieve the blueprints or face dire consequences. With a mountain of gambling debt looming, I felt I had no choice but to proceed. I kept low as I approached the hangar.

Just as I reached it, I saw you and your friend Matt securing your airship. I pressed myself against the building, my heart pounding. That's when you looked up, and our eyes met.

"Matthew," you called urgently, "there's someone in here! After him!"

My heart leaped into my throat. I bolted, heading into the woods, knowing you and Matt were hot on my heels. I could hear your footsteps closing in. Desperation took hold, and I reached into my pocket, pulling out one of the smoke bombs the man had given me. Just as you were about to catch me, I threw it.

Thick smoke billowed, filling the air. I held my breath and dashed into the cover of the trees. I could hear coughing and stumbling behind me. When I saw you hit the ground, I knew it was my chance. I circled back, slipping into the hangar, hoping you were only unconscious, not worse.

Once inside, I made a beeline for the workshop at the back. It was a treasure trove of blueprints and gadgets. I pulled out the small camera—the fancy piece of equipment the man had provided—and started snapping photos. Click after click, I documented everything I could: each blueprint, every design. Guilt gnawed at me, but fear of my debtor's threats kept me going.

I didn't need to hurry. Those smoke bombs were potent, and I knew you'd be out cold for hours if you woke up at all. I took my time, ensuring clear shots of every detail. As I worked, the ticking clock on the wall was the only sound breaking the silence, a constant reminder of time slipping away.

Finally, I had all the photos I needed. I packed up my camera, taking one last look around the workshop. Guilt weighed heavily, but I had to get out of there. I slipped away the way I came, moving through the shadows until I was clear of the ranch.

****

Edwin's voice wavered as he finished his story. "I didn't want to do it, but I had no choice. He threatened me, and I... I was desperate."

Jedidiah's grip on Edwin's collar tightened for a moment before he let go, stepping back. His eyes were hard, but there was a flicker of understanding. "You could have come to us for help," he said, his voice stern but not without compassion.

Edwin looked down, his shoulders slumping in shame. "I didn't think you would believe me. And I didn't want to put anyone in danger."

Jedidiah shook his head, a mix of frustration and sympathy crossing his face as he tried to process the betrayal and fear that Edwin must have felt. "We need to focus on finding Phineas and Myra," he finally said, his tone firm. "And we'll deal with the rest later."

Edwin nodded, relieved but still tense, his posture straightening. "I'll help in any way I can," he said earnestly.

Jedidiah turned back to the blueprints, his mind racing with the implications of what Edwin had revealed. "Let's get what we need and get back to the others. We don't have much time," he said, his eyes scanning the designs with renewed urgency.

Jedidiah picked up the crate and started for the

door, his jaw set in determination. Just as they were about to leave, the first automaton reentered the room through the enormous double doors. "Stop!" He ordered them, his mechanical voice echoing in the room.

Ready to fight his way out, Davenport set the crate down and squared his shoulders. "I'm just taking what's mine!" he declared, his eyes blazing with defiance.

"You are for...getting the ultra...sonic dis...ruptor can...non," the mechanical man said, walking further into the room with stiff, deliberate movements, pulling the large weapon behind him. Its wheels creaked under the weight as the automaton moved it into place, the polished metal gleaming in the dim light of the shop.

Jedidiah was in complete awe as he spotted the monstrous contraption. To others, it might have looked like a pile of junk, but to him, it was a masterful piece of art. "You had a fully assembled one just sitting in the storage room?" he asked in disbelief.

"That would be cor...rect," the automaton replied simply.

Jedidiah glanced over at Edwin, who merely shrugged, just as confused. He turned back to the mechanical man and said, "I don't have to ask questions. We'll take it!"

"Your to...tal will be eight thou...sand of your

Amer...ican dol...lars," the automaton stated.

"Eight thousand dollars?" Jedidiah stammered, his eyes widening.

The automaton didn't waver as he said, "Five thou...sand for the can...non, three thou...sand for the blue...prints."

"Half of these blueprints are mine!" Jedidiah shouted, his face flushing with anger. He quickly changed his tone as he saw the first automaton communicate with the second one through a series of eye flickers. The second mechanical man approached, and together, they effortlessly lifted the ultrasonic disruptor cannon. One automaton lifted the front end while the other lifted the back end. In perfect synchronization, they stepped up onto the wooden sidewalk and carefully set the cannon down before reentering the store.

"Gosh!" Edwin exclaimed, his eyes wide with awe. "That thing must weigh a ton!"

Jedidiah glanced at young Bancroft for a moment, his brow furrowing as he took in the impressive strength of these two machines. Realizing a confrontation would be pointless, he turned back to the first mechanical man. "Eight thousand, you say? Will you take a bank draft?" he asked.

While the newly purchased cannon was being loaded onto the Swift, Matthew was guiding the Icarus toward Toronto, intent on intercepting

Jedidiah and Edwin. His mind raced with urgency, knowing they had little time to lose. He hoped Tom was still safe and that their plan would come together in time.

As Matthew scanned the horizon, he was relieved to spot the Swift about halfway between Toronto and their previous landing site. He signaled frantically from the deck, hoping to catch Jedidiah's attention.

With the aid of his special goggles, Jedidiah recognized the Icarus. Finding a clearing, both ships descended, and moments later, the three of them rendezvoused.

"Matthew!" Jedidiah exclaimed, a mix of relief and confusion in his voice. "What's going on? Did you find them?"

Matthew, slightly out of breath from running over, said, "They're at a warehouse near the harbor in Whitby. I left Tom behind to keep an eye on things, but I'm worried he might have run into trouble."

Jedidiah's face hardened with resolve. "We need to move quickly. Are you sure they'll still be there when we get back?"

"We did what we could to delay their takeoff," Matthew explained. "But no guarantees. That's why we have to hurry. Did you get the parts and blueprints for the weapon?"

Jedidiah smiled as he said, "We did better than

that."

"We got the whole cannon!" Edwin jumped excitedly.

"Excellent!" Matthew shouted as he turned to rush back to the Icarus. "Follow me, I'll lead the way!"

Minutes later, the two airships were hovering close to the warehouses by the Whitby harbor. Using semaphore signals to communicate from ship to ship, Jedidiah and Matthew each landed their vessels one more time so they could assess the area before setting their plan into motion.

"Let's find Tom first," Matthew suggested. "He can let us know what's been going on!" He quietly began to creep his way along the grounds, leading the way to where he last saw the young man. Suddenly, he let out a gasp as he spotted a prone figure lying face down with a broken piece of wood beside it. "Tom!" Matthew Colton shouted.

CHAPTER XV

The Rescue

"Tom!" Matthew screamed as he rushed over to the figure lying on the ground. His hands were tied behind his back, and ropes secured his ankles.

"Matt!" a voice called from behind a set of crates near the building.

Everyone turned to see Tom Miller waving to them from his hiding spot. They rolled the person on the ground over and saw that it was definitely not their young friend but a complete stranger.

"If you're over there," Matthew asked, stunned, "who is this?" He immediately checked the stranger's pulse and breathed a sigh of relief as he realized he was still alive.

Tom shrugged. "Just some fellow that attacked me!"

"Attacked you?" Jedidiah asked as he and Matthew rushed over and knelt behind the crates.

Edwin Bancroft immediately followed their

actions and smugly asked, "So, you did that to him?"

"Who else?" Tom smiled proudly.

Jedidiah looked at Tom with a mix of admiration and curiosity. "How did you manage to take him down?"

Tom's smile faded slightly as he remembered the intensity of the encounter. His mind drifted back to just after Matthew Colton departed.

✳✳✳✳✳✳✳✳✳✳✳✳✳✳✳✳✳✳✳✳

As Tom Miller watched the Icarus flying away, he remained oblivious to the danger lurking behind him. Suddenly, a movement in the corner of his eye caught his attention. He turned just in time to see a man lunging at him, swinging a wooden axe handle directly at his head!

Tom barely had enough time to react. He raised his arms in a futile attempt to block the blow. The handle swung toward him, causing him to instinctively stumble backward on the loose gravel. He fell to the ground, narrowly dodging the handle as it whizzed past his face by mere inches.

Growling in frustration, the attacker swung again, aiming for Tom's prone form. Tom rolled aside just in time, the handle striking the ground with a dull thud. He scrambled to his feet, heart pounding in his chest.

Tom Miller watching the Icarus flying away,
oblivious to the danger lurking behind him.

The attacker swung once more, but Tom ducked, the handle slicing through the air above him. His eyes darted around, searching for anything to defend himself with. Spotting a loose plank of wood nearby, he lunged for it and gripped it tightly.

With the man charging at him, swinging the handle wildly, Tom used the plank as a makeshift shield, deflecting the blow. The impact sent vibrations up his arms, but he managed to hold his ground.

Snarling, the attacker swung low this time. Tom jumped back, narrowly avoiding the handle by a hair's breadth. Desperation fueled a wild swing with the plank, which by sheer luck connected with the man's side.

The attacker grunted in pain but persisted, swinging again. Tom barely managed to block it with the plank, the force knocking him off balance and sending him tumbling to the ground once more.

Seizing his chance, the attacker raised the handle for a final, decisive strike. Thinking quickly, Tom grabbed a handful of dirt and flung it into the man's face. The attacker recoiled, rubbing his eyes.

Tom used this to his advantage. He turned to run away. As he did, he squeezed his eyes shut in fear and threw the plank behind him with all his might. By sheer accident, the plank connected with the side of the man's head. The attacker collapsed to the ground, unconscious.

Breathing heavily, Tom took a moment to steady himself. He glanced around, making sure no one else was nearby. Spotting some rope lying on a crate, he quickly tied the attacker's hands and feet. Satisfied the area was clear, he hurried back to his hiding spot, heart still racing.

****

"After I took the axe handle away from the brute, I engaged him in some bare-knuckle boxing." Tom's version of the story was a bit more embellished compared to the actual events. "Finally, he was on his knees begging for mercy. I took pity on him and knocked him out cold with a final blow!" He held up his fist and smiled triumphantly.

"That's amazing!" Matthew exclaimed.

Tom merely shrugged. "I just did what I had to do."

Jedidiah nodded, impressed. "You did well, Tom."

Edwin Bancroft, on the other hand, was less than impressed. "Why do I feel like that's not quite how it happened?"

"Why would you say that?" Tom became immediately defensive.

Edwin shrugged. "I just don't see a kid like you taking on a brute like him."

"Well, I did!" Tom shouted defensively. "And stop calling me a kid!"

Young Bancroft pointed toward the ground next to the man and asked, "If you knocked him out with your fist, where did that plank come from?"

At this point, both Jedidiah and Matthew stepped in. They patted Miller on the back. "Glad you're safe, Tom, but we still have a rescue to complete," Jedidiah said, his voice firm with resolve.

With a sense of urgency in his voice, Matthew asked. "Have you spotted Phineas or Myra anymore since I've been gone?"

Tom nodded. "I watched the guards remove them from the airship and take them back inside the warehouse. He's the only one in there with them. The rest are aboard the airship, helping their leader with the plague mask repair the damage we did to the engine."

Jedidiah's eyes narrowed with determination. "Alright, here's the plan. I'll take the Swift up and aim the ultrasonic disruptor cannon I just bought at them. They should feel the same effects we did when they used theirs against us."

Matthew nodded, understanding. "While you're doing that, Tom, Edwin, and I will sneak into the warehouse, take out the guard, and rescue Professor Hargroves and Ms. Bancroft."

Tom's face lit up with a mix of excitement and

apprehension. "Then we make a mad dash to the Icarus and join you in the sky?"

"Exactly," Jedidiah confirmed. "We don't have much time. Let's move."

With the plan set, Jedidiah quickly boarded his airship, its engines roaring to life as it lifted off the ground. Matthew, Tom, and Edwin crouched low, moving stealthily towards the warehouse. The tension was almost unbearable, each step bringing them closer to their goal and the danger that awaited.

As the Swift ascended into the sky, Jedidiah adjusted the controls, his eyes fixed on the enemy airship below. He could see the figures moving about, oblivious to the impending attack. He positioned himself directly above the vessel, ensuring a clear shot with the ultrasonic disruptor cannon.

Down below, Matthew, Tom, and Edwin crept closer to the warehouse. They moved silently, using the shadows and crates for cover. Tom pointed to a side entrance, and they quickly made their way over. Matthew carefully eased the door open, peeking inside to ensure the coast was clear.

Inside the warehouse, Phineas and Myra were bound and seated on the floor, guarded by a single man. The guard paced back and forth, occasionally glancing towards the door. He seemed agitated, unaware of the rescue team closing in.

Matthew motioned for Tom and Edwin to follow him. They slipped through the door, moving quietly towards the guard. Tom's heart pounded in his chest, his grip tightening on the plank he grabbed from beside the other man. Edwin held a length of rope, ready to use it.

As they neared the guard, Matthew signaled for them to stop. He picked up a small pebble and tossed it across the room. The pebble clattered against the wall, drawing the guard's attention. The guard turned, stepping away from Phineas and Myra to investigate the noise.

Seizing the moment, Matthew lunged at the man, tackling him to the ground. The guard struggled, but Matthew held him down. Tom and Edwin quickly joined in, helping to subdue him. Tom wildly swung the plank and knocked the man out cold.

"I knew you didn't use your first!" Edwin exclaimed triumphantly.

Before Tom could reply, Matthew shouted, "Get them untied," pointing towards the captives while keeping an eye on the unconscious guard.

Edwin and Tom rushed over to Phineas and Myra, quickly untying their bonds and removing their gags. Myra looked up at them, relief washing over her face. Then, her eyes fell on Edwin, and she gasped in surprise.

"Edwin? What are you doing here?" Myra

asked, her voice filled with shock and confusion.

"Aunt Myra, I'll explain everything later," Edwin replied hurriedly.

Myra nodded, her mind racing with questions.

"We need to move fast," Phineas added, rubbing his wrists where the ropes had chafed them. "Whatever you've done to distract them won't keep them busy forever."

Matthew merely smiled as he mysteriously said, "Oh, I think they'll be immobilized for quite some time."

Outside, the Swift hovered ominously above the enemy airship. Jedidiah aimed the disruptor cannon, his finger hovering over the trigger. The steam engine powering it hummed surprisingly softly. With a deep breath, he fired. The cannon emitted a powerful burst of ultrasonic waves, directed at the grounded vessel.

The effect was immediate. The enemy airship shuddered, and the crew members clutched their heads, disoriented by the intense vibrations. The masked leader stumbled, struggling to maintain control as the disruptor waves washed over them.

Matthew, Tom, Edwin, Phineas, and Myra dashed out of the warehouse, heading for the Icarus. The air was filled with the sounds of chaos as the disruptor cannon did its work. The group reached the Icarus, clambering aboard and starting the engines.

"Hold on!" Matthew shouted as the Icarus lifted off the ground, joining the Swift in the sky. They soared upwards, escaping the reach of their enemies.

Safely away from danger, Matthew used the semaphore flags near the helm to signal to Jedidiah that everyone was safe. Suddenly realizing he had taken complete control of Phineas' ship, he turned and asked the eccentric older man if he would like to take the wheel.

Phineas B. Hargroves merely smiled as he said, "My dear boy, you're doing just fine. Just get us out of here!"

The two airships flew in close formation, heading away from the warehouse and the chaos below. The wind whipped past them, carrying away the tension of the rescue and filling them with a sense of triumph and relief. They set a direct course to the field where they had left the Enigma earlier that morning.

As the warehouses were disappearing from view, Myra Wilhelmina Bancroft turned to her nephew, her eyes filled with a mix of relief and confusion. "Edwin, what on earth is going on? How did you get involved in all this?" she demanded to know for the second time.

Edwin took a deep breath. "It's a long story, Aunt Myra, but I promise I'll tell you everything as soon as we're out of danger."

Tom Miller suddenly stepped forward and said, "I can tell you, Ms. Bancroft!"

Matthew immediately turned from the helm and, with both hands, pulled the younger man towards him. "How about you just help me navigate for now?"

Tom sighed and agreed, disappointed that he wasn't allowed to say what he wanted.

After landing the two vessels, Myra and Edwin quickly boarded the Enigma, while Matthew transferred over to the Swift, leaving Phineas and Tom to manage the Icarus. With renewed determination, the three vessels set a course for Toronto, the second checkpoint of the race.

The short journey after this was uneventful, and by 2 PM, the trio of airships descended upon the bustling city. As they landed, they were greeted by a crowd of spectators and race officials. The atmosphere was charged with excitement and curiosity.

Jedidiah, Phineas, and Myra disembarked, heading toward the checkpoint office. They were surprised to learn that Captain Jonathan "Jack" Braddock and Sir Reginald Fortescue had only left Toronto about thirty minutes prior, delayed by more unexplained issues with their airships. Professor Thaddeus Montgomery had departed two hours earlier, his ship traveling at half speed due to ongoing repairs that he hoped to complete en route to the next checkpoint in London.

The officials handed over the steel versions of the falcon statues, the second token in their journey. The miniatures were exquisite, capturing the essence of the larger statue, though one detail was missing.

"These miniatures don't have the monocle like the full-sized version," Phineas remarked, inspecting his statue closely.

A nearby official overheard and replied with a smile, "They're close enough, sir. Nobody will notice if you don't point it out."

Jedidiah, Myra, and Phineas exchanged amused glances, appreciating the attention to detail that had gone into the race's unique rewards. With the steel falcons in hand, they felt a renewed sense of purpose and determination.

After a brief rest and refueling of their airships, they gathered for a final check before departure. The sky above Toronto was clear, the perfect backdrop for the next leg of their journey.

As everyone returned to their respective vessels, Jedidiah turned to Matthew and said, "On to the next checkpoint. Hopefully, our troubles won't follow us into the United Kingdom."

Matthew Colton nodded in agreement, aware of the dangers that still lurked. The engines roared to life once more, and the three airships lifted into the sky, heading toward their next destination.

As they soared through the clouds, the anticipation of what lay ahead mixed with the relief of their successful rescue. They knew the journey to London would be challenging, but with their combined strength and determination, they were ready to face whatever obstacles came their way.

After they were thousands of feet in the air, safely on the deck of the Enigma, Myra Wilhelmina Bancroft turned to her nephew and for the third time demanded to know how he got involved in all of this.

Edwin glanced up and nodded. He took a deep breath, the weight of his experiences evident on his face. "It all started..."

CHAPTER XVI

Crossing the Atlantic

As the journey from Toronto to London began, Jedidiah stood on the deck of the Swift next to the helm, his eyes focused on the maps and charts spread out before him. The gentle hum of the airship's engines provided a constant background noise as they sailed smoothly through the sky. He glanced at his pocket watch and sighed, the weight of the upcoming journey pressing heavily on his mind.

Matthew, noticing Jedidiah's expression, walked over with a concerned look. "What's wrong, Jed?" he asked, his voice cutting through the steady drone of the engines.

Jedidiah looked up from the charts, meeting Matthew's eyes with a serious expression. "We're about to enter one of the most dangerous parts of the race," he explained, his tone heavy with concern. "In about 24 hours, we'll be leaving land behind and spending the next two and a half days traveling over the ocean."

Matthew's eyes widened in surprise. "Two and a half days? I didn't realize it was going to take that long."

Jedidiah nodded, his gaze returning to the maps. "The Atlantic Ocean is huge and unpredictable. We'll be at the mercy of the elements with no land in sight. It's a treacherous part of the journey, but it's the only way to reach London in time."

Matthew took a deep breath, absorbing the gravity of the situation. "What do we need to do to prepare?" he asked, his voice steady despite the unease he felt.

Jedidiah pointed to the charts. "We need to make sure our navigation is precise. Any deviation could lead us off course, and out there, it would be nearly impossible to correct. We also need to check and double-check all our equipment. The disruptor cannon, the engines, and the airbag—all of it needs to be in top condition."

Matthew nodded, determined. "Aye aye, Captain!" He smiled as he saluted.

Jedidiah returned the smile, albeit briefly, before turning his attention back to the preparations.

On the Icarus, Tom was busy assisting Phineas. The eccentric older man was muttering to himself as he fine-tuned the engine. "Tom, make sure the stabilizers are functioning perfectly. We can't afford any mishaps over the ocean."

Tom nodded determination in his eyes. "Consider it done, Professor."

Meanwhile, on the Enigma, Myra and Edwin were performing ongoing inspections of their vessel. Edwin was going over the engines, his hands moving with practiced precision. "Aunt Myra, everything is in good shape. We shouldn't have any problems." Exhausted, he turned to her and said, "I don't think we need to constantly double-check everything."

Myra nodded, her face set with determination. "I understand what you're saying, Edwin. However, we never know when some sneaky little saboteur," she aimed that remark directly at him, "might have done some type of time-delayed vandalism to my ship."

"I've already told you, Aunt Myra," the young man replied, irritated despite his shame. "I never once touched any of the airships."

"But you were going to and that's bad enough!" She huffed as she turned her gaze towards the open sky. Unlike before, where each ship took a slightly different route to the next checkpoint, the three airships planned to stay pretty close together over the next few days until they reached the United Kingdom.

As the hours passed, the sun dipped below the

horizon, casting a warm glow over the landscape. The three airships sailed steadily, their course set for the vast expanse of the Atlantic.

Later that night, as the stars began to shine, Jedidiah and Matthew gathered on the deck of the Swift. After spending hours on constant checks of their equipment, they realized there wasn't much else they could do but sit back and enjoy the ride.

Matthew clapped his old childhood friend on the shoulder and said, "We're going to make it, Jed."

On the Icarus, Tom and Phineas also stood on the deck watching the night sky. "We have a long journey ahead, Tom," Phineas said, his voice thoughtful. "But I have faith in our skills and our airships."

Tom grinned, his confidence bolstered by Phineas' words. "We'll get through this, Professor. Just wait—we'll end up winning the race!"

On the Enigma, Myra Wilhelmina Bancroft and her nephew Edwin stood side by side, their eyes fixed on the horizon. Edwin turned to his aunt and said, "I'm sorry I got myself in a situation to be blackmailed and forced to do unthinkable acts." The sincerity in his voice was undeniable.

"You're right," he continued. "Even though I never committed any of the sabotage, I fully intended to. And stealing all of Mr. Davenport's designs was also one of the lowest points in my life."

"That gambling debt must have been really bad for you to be forced into something like this," Myra remarked, a touch of compassion in her eyes. "I just don't understand why you didn't come to me. How much could you possibly owe?"

Edwin took a deep breath as he prepared to tell his aunt one final, horrible truth. "Aunt Myra, you know how two years ago when I turned eighteen, you put the Enigma in my name?"

Ms. Bancroft nodded. "That was in case anything happened to me. It would go to you as my only living relative." Her eyes suddenly widened as it dawned on her. "Oh, Edwin! You didn't?"

"Now you see why I had to do what I was told," he said, turning his face away from the eccentric older woman in shame. Turning back, he added, "Aunt Myra, he was going to take the Enigma from you, and I couldn't let that happen!"

Myra Wilhelmina Bancroft became silent for a moment as she thought everything over. She finally smiled as she looked back at her nephew. "Well then, we'll just have to make sure we win the race. The prize money will be more than enough to pay off your debt to that scoundrel, whoever he is!"

Edwin nodded, his heart swelling with pride. "I won't let you down, Aunt Myra."

To show her determination, Ms. Bancroft pushed the throttle forward slightly, increasing her lead on both the Swift and the Icarus.

They spent most of the next day traveling over the landmass of Canada. Shortly after five o'clock on the evening of Wednesday, September 7th, 1881, they embarked on their oceanic voyage.

The next two and a half days of the journey went by uneventfully. Occasionally, the crew of each ship would use semaphore flags to communicate, updating each other about their conditions.

Finally, after over fifty-seven hours with only deep blue seawater beneath them, on Saturday, September 9th, 1881, at 7:30 AM local time, they reached land.

Jedidiah was awake, keeping a vigilant watch at the helm. The dim light from the instruments cast a soft glow on his face as he scanned the horizon. His heart leaped with relief when he spotted the dark outline of the Irish coast.

"Land ho!" he called out softly, not wanting to disturb Matthew, who was asleep in the cabin behind him. The young man had been exhausted after the long, stressful days of travel, and Jedidiah knew he needed his rest.

Davenport allowed himself a brief moment of satisfaction, knowing they had successfully navigated the treacherous oceanic crossing. But there was still a long way to go.

Meanwhile, on the Icarus, Tom was trying to

stay alert as he assisted Phineas. His eyes were heavy with fatigue, but he fought to keep them open. He knew how important it was to maintain vigilance during this critical part of their journey.

Phineas, who had been taking a brief nap to recharge, stirred at the sound of Tom's soft exclamation. "Professor, I think I see land!"

Professor Hargroves began rubbing his eyes and peering out into the darkness. A smile spread across his face as he saw the faint outline of the coast. "Well done, Tom. Let's keep our course steady. We still have a long trip to the next checkpoint."

On the Enigma, Myra Wilhelmina Bancroft was awake, unable to sleep due to worry about their journey and her nephew. She paced the deck of the ship, her thoughts racing. The stress of the trip and the burden of Edwin's involvement in the sabotage weighed heavily on her mind, not to mention the dread of potentially losing her airship.

As the coastline came into view, she felt a surge of relief. "We made it!" she called out quietly, her voice tinged with a mix of exhaustion and determination.

Edwin, exhausted from the emotional and physical strain of the trip, had been sleeping soundly. Her call stirred him, and he groggily made his way to the deck. "Aunt Myra, we're over land?"

Myra nodded, a small smile breaking through her worried expression. "Yes, Edwin. We're over land again. But we still have a long way to go. Get some more rest; we'll need all our strength for the final leg."

The three airships continued their journey throughout the night. Eventually, the sun rose, casting a warm glow over the landscape. This part of the journey had been much smoother. The crews of each ship continued to take turns resting and manning their posts.

Several hours later, with the sun now high in the sky, Jedidiah called a brief meeting with the captains of the other two ships. Using semaphore flags, he relayed instructions for their final approach to London.

As the airships neared their destination, the tension among them grew. Each ship was in top condition, and the competition was fierce. They all knew that the third checkpoint would be a critical moment in the race.

Finally, at 8:30 PM local time, the three airships began their descent towards the University of London. Despite the later hour, the campus was a hive of activity, with students and faculty gathered to witness the arrival of the race participants.

Jedidiah, Phineas, and Myra disembarked, greeted by a crowd of spectators and university officials. They were directed toward the checkpoint, where they would receive the next set of miniature statues.

As they approached the checkpoint, Jedidiah's eyes were drawn to a memorial plaque near the entrance of the main building. It was dedicated to Jonathan Blake.

Phineas and Myra paused in front of the memorial, their expressions somber. Myra reached out and touched the plaque, her fingers tracing the engraved letters.

"It still feels like it was just yesterday," Myra said softly, her voice tinged with sadness.

Phineas nodded, his eyes distant. "We were so close. If only we hadn't been so competitive..."

Myra sighed. "We both blamed each other for what happened. But in the end, it was just a tragic accident."

****

The memory of that day was still vivid. Phineas and Myra had been on an expedition in the mountains, competing to see who could reach the summit first. Jonathan had been with them, always the mediator, trying to keep the peace.

It was a clear, crisp morning as they set out from their base camp. The sky was a brilliant blue, and the snow-covered peaks glistened in the sunlight. Phineas and Myra were in high spirits, their competitive natures driving them forward. Jonathan, ever the voice of reason, walked between

A memorial plaque
dedicated to Jonathan Blake.

them, his calm demeanor a stark contrast to their enthusiasm.

As they ascended, the terrain grew steeper and more treacherous. The air was thin, and every step was a challenge. But neither Phineas nor Myra would back down. They exchanged playful taunts, each trying to outdo the other. Jonathan watched them with a mix of amusement and concern, cautioning them to be mindful of the conditions.

"We should slow down," Jonathan said, his breath visible in the cold air. "The snow looks unstable. We need to be careful."

Phineas laughed, waving off Jonathan's concerns. "We'll be fine, old friend. Just a bit further and we'll reach the summit."

Myra smirked, her competitive spirit flaring. "Don't tell me you're afraid of a little snow, Jonathan."

Jonathan shook his head, his expression serious. "It's not about fear, Myra. It's about safety. We need to stay alert."

Ignoring his advice, Phineas and Myra pressed on, their rivalry blinding them to the danger. The snow beneath their feet crunched with every step, a subtle warning they failed to heed. Jonathan followed closely, his eyes scanning the slope for any signs of trouble.

As they neared the top, the competition grew fiercer. Myra surged ahead, determined to beat

Phineas. Not to be outdone, Phineas quickened his pace, his focus solely on reaching the summit first. Jonathan's warnings grew more urgent, but they fell on deaf ears.

Suddenly, the ground beneath them began to shift. A deep rumble echoed through the mountains, and the snow started to slide. In their haste, Phineas and Myra had triggered an avalanche.

"Run!" Jonathan shouted, his voice filled with panic.

Phineas and Myra turned, their faces pale with fear. The roaring wave of snow and ice would be upon them in seconds. Jonathan pushed them both forward, trying to get them to safety. But the avalanche was too fast, too powerful.

Jonathan was caught in the middle, swept away by the unstoppable force. Phineas and Myra scrambled to the side, barely escaping the full brunt of the avalanche. They watched in horror as their friend disappeared beneath the churning mass of snow.

When the avalanche finally subsided, the silence was deafening. Phineas and Myra were left standing on the mountainside, their hearts pounding with shock and terror.

"Jonathan!" Myra screamed, her voice echoing through the valley. "Jonathan, where are you?"

Phineas grabbed her arm, his face etched with guilt. "We have to find him. He can't be gone."

For days, they searched tirelessly, digging through the snow and calling out Jonathan's name. But there was no sign of him. The mountain had claimed him, leaving them with nothing but their grief and regret.

Eventually, they had to accept the harsh reality that he was gone. The loss of their friend left a deep scar, one that time could never fully heal. They blamed themselves and each other, their once-strong friendship strained by the weight of their guilt.

****

Phineas shook his head as if trying to dispel the painful memories. His eyes were clouded with sorrow. "Jonathan was a brilliant man," he said quietly. "He didn't deserve what happened to him."

Myra nodded, her gaze distant as she stared at the plaque. "I just hope he's at peace," she murmured, her voice tinged with sadness.

Phineas B. Hargroves thought for a moment, his brow furrowing with hesitation. He turned to the older woman, his expression earnest. "Listen, there's something I need to tell you," he said, his voice tinged with urgency.

Myra looked at him, curiosity lighting up her eyes. "Go ahead," she encouraged, sensing the importance of his words.

Phineas hesitated, his fingers fidgeting with the edge of his coat. "You're going to think I'm crazy," he began, his voice wavering slightly. "And maybe I am. You know how the mind can play tricks on you."

Myra's impatience grew, and she crossed her arms, tapping her foot. "Stop beating around the bush!" she demanded, her tone sharp. "Just tell me."

Phineas took a deep breath, his eyes locking onto hers. "You're going to think I was seeing a ghost, but..."

Just as he was about to finally say it, Edwin walked over, his expression a mix of shock and recognition. He glanced at the plaque and then pointed at the photo, his eyes widening. "That's the man who's been blackmailing me!"

CHAPTER XVII

Unexpected Revelation

"He's what?" Myra asked in shocked disbelief.

"He's the man who's been blackmailing me!" Edwin repeated, his voice trembling with a mix of fear and anger.

"Who is?" The older eccentric woman's face shone with confusion.

Phineas took a step closer, his eyes narrowing. "Jonathan Blake," he said quietly. "I saw his face when he removed his mask during the attack. I couldn't believe it then, but now... it all makes sense."

"Is that what you were about to tell me?" Myra's eyes widened as she looked between Phineas and Edwin. "Are you both trying to tell me that Jonathan Blake is alive?"

Phineas nodded, his expression grim. "He must have survived the avalanche and somehow made his way back."

"This doesn't make sense!" Myra turned and looked back at the plaque with their old friend's photo. "Why didn't he ever reach out to either of us? Why didn't he let us know he was alive?"

"I don't know," Phineas admitted, unable to answer the question. "Perhaps he held a grudge against us and blamed us for the accident."

"We certainly blamed each other enough over the years," Myra remarked. "I just can't believe he's been behind all the vandalism and sabotage."

Phineas' face darkened as he glanced at Edwin, truly acknowledging him for the first time. "And he used your gambling debts to force you into his schemes."

Edwin nodded, regret evident on his face. "And worst of all, thanks to my debt he..."

Myra shook her head at her nephew, signaling him to stop talking. She didn't want anyone to know that everything she owned was on the line. She looked back to Phineas and said, "I guess we owe each other an apology. I know *I* owe *you* one." With genuine sincerity, she said, "I'm so sorry, Phineas. Can you ever forgive me?"

Phineas B. Hargroves softened more than anyone had ever seen before as he said, "My dear woman, only if you can forgive *me*."

Jedidiah, who had been listening intently, stepped forward. "So this is what the trouble has been between the two of you all these years?"

Phineas nodded, admitting that they both had behaved like fools. "We tried to remain partners after the accident. Our friendship was obviously over and buried along with Jonathan Blake."

"Our resentment towards each other was just too great," Myra added. "We ended up sabotaging each other's inventions and breakthroughs over the next couple of years until we finally decided to part ways."

"We'd see each other in passing at different events, but it was never the same again," Phineas stated.

Jedidiah took a deep breath, absorbing the gravity of the revelations. "I know it's hard for the two of you to comprehend, but at least now we know who we're dealing with."

As they continued to stand there, absorbing the gravity of the situation, a race official approached them.

"Excuse me," he said, motioning with the clipboard in his hand. "The check-in booth is just a few hundred yards that way." He pointed towards the table in question. "The three of you need to check in and collect your falcon statue so you can continue to your next checkpoint."

"Thank you, we'll do that," Jedidiah nodded, turning to the others. "Let's go see where we stand and how far behind we are now."

As they made their way to the booth, where a

small crowd had gathered, Phineas turned to Myra and casually asked, "Is Edwin your sister Rebecca's son?"

Myra gave a brief, almost imperceptible nod. "Yes, he is."

Phineas' expression softened for a moment, a flicker of understanding passing between them before they reached the booth. The official greeted them warmly.

"Welcome! Congratulations on making it this far," the official said, handing each of them a solid copper miniature, the second statue and third token of their journey. "You are now officially checked in and free to continue to Paris."

Jedidiah glanced around. "Are any of the other contestants still here, or have they already left?"

The official checked his clipboard. "Captain Jonathan 'Jack' Braddock and Sir Reginald Fortescue left about thirty minutes ago. Professor Thaddeus Montgomery departed two hours earlier, though his ship is still undergoing repairs."

"Thank you," Jedidiah replied, a determined look in his eyes. "We'll be on our way soon as well."

As they moved away from the booth, Matthew spoke up. "We need a better way to communicate between our ships. Relying on semaphore flags isn't going to cut it, especially as the competition heats up."

Jedidiah nodded thoughtfully. "You're right. We need a more efficient system."

"Why not use your auto telegraph?" Matthew suggested. "It works well for long-distance communication."

Phineas shook his head immediately. "We'd have to connect wires between the ships every time we needed to send a message. It's not practical while we're in flight."

Myra, listening intently, chimed in. "What about the telephone? It's becoming quite popular around the world."

Jedidiah considered this for a moment, then shook his head. "That would still involve stretching wires across the air from ship to ship."

Suddenly, an idea sparked in Jedidiah's mind. His eyes lit up with excitement. "But what if we could do it wirelessly?"

Matthew and Myra both looked intrigued. "Wirelessly?" Myra repeated. "How would that work?"

Jedidiah began to pace, his mind racing with possibilities. "If we could send and receive signals through the air, like a telegraph but without the wires, we could communicate in real-time. We need to brainstorm how we can make this work."

Phineas nodded, his enthusiasm growing. "Maybe we can use radio waves. I've read about experiments with wireless telegraphy."

Jedidiah's eyes widened. "Yes, that's it! We can use radio waves to transmit our messages. We just need to design a transmitter and receiver that can operate reliably on our airships."

"As long as we're working on this design, why not fully incorporate all of our ideas?" Myra eagerly suggested. "Instead of just transmitting messages wirelessly, let's integrate the design of the telephone and transmit our voices wirelessly."

Phineas, despite his earlier reservations, couldn't help but be intrigued by the idea. "It would require some sophisticated engineering, but it could work. We'll need to create a stable frequency and ensure the signal is strong enough to travel between the ships."

"We should also consider the range and how to keep the signal clear despite any interference," Myra added.

Jedidiah nodded, already sketching out ideas in a notebook he grabbed from the check-in booth. "We'll need to work together on this. Matthew, you, Tom, and Edwin can go gather parts, starting with three telephones to dismantle." Jedidiah handed Matthew some cash. "Find the nearest phone company and hurry!"

"The Post Office Telegraph should have what you need!" Myra remarked as she quickly scribbled out a list of supplies they would require. Phineas did the same, and the young man took off down the street with Tom and Edwin in tow.

Suddenly, a thought struck Jedidiah, and he asked the eccentric older woman, "Will they be open this late?"

She merely shrugged her shoulders and replied, "Someone has to be watching the switchboard!"

Phineas, despite himself, smiled at their enthusiasm. "We might not be the first to attempt this, but we're certainly the most energetic group to do so."

The three airship captains huddled together, exchanging ideas and drawing up plans. They decided to check the crate Jedidiah had purchased earlier, hoping to find designs or parts that could assist in their endeavor. To their delight, they discovered a set of blueprints for a basic wireless transmitter and receiver, along with various electrical components that could be repurposed.

As they worked, Matthew, Tom, and Edwin navigated the bustling streets of London, the gas lamps casting a warm glow over the cobblestones as they hurried along. The city was alive with activity despite the late hour. Carriages rattled by, and the clatter of horse hooves echoed through the narrow streets. Street vendors hawked their wares, and the aroma of roasted chestnuts mingled with the damp, cool air.

"We need to make this quick," Matthew said, glancing around. "The Post Office Telegraph is just a few blocks away."

As they walked, Edwin Bancroft couldn't help but cast a sideways glance at Tom Miller. "Try not to slow us down, kid. We can't afford any more delays."

Tom groaned at the remark but chose not to react. "Just worry about yourself, Bancroft."

The tension between them was so thick you could cut it with a knife. Matthew cringed, hoping it wouldn't come to blows. As they navigated through the crowded streets, they passed by the imposing façade of the British Museum, which loomed over Great Russell Street.

Outside the museum, Matthew noticed a group of men in dark suits and bowler hats. Their stern expressions and watchful eyes marked them as detectives from Scotland Yard. They were speaking with museum staff, their presence indicating the seriousness of the recent theft of an ancient relic. The detectives moved methodically, questioning witnesses and examining the scene, their reputation as skilled investigators adding intensity to the investigation.

Continuing their stroll, the iconic St. Paul's Cathedral came into view, its dome silhouetted against the night sky. Finally reaching the Post Office Telegraph building, they found a clerk still on duty, his tired eyes widening with surprise at the late-night visitors.

"What can I do for you gentlemen?" he asked, adjusting his spectacles.

Matthew stepped forward. "We need three telephones to dismantle for parts. It's urgent."

The clerk raised an eyebrow, suspicion evident in his gaze. "Telephones, you say? And for dismantling? I'm afraid we don't just hand out equipment to anyone off the street, especially for something as drastic as dismantling."

Tom, sensing the clerk's hesitation, tried to assert himself. "Look, we don't have time for questions. We're in the middle of a very important race, and we need those parts."

The clerk crossed his arms, unimpressed. "A race, you say? And why should I believe that? These are expensive pieces of equipment, not toys to be handed out on a whim."

Edwin, trying a different approach, stepped forward and mentioned the cash Jedidiah had given them. "We're willing to pay for the telephones, but please, we don't have much time."

Matthew held up the money to show they were telling the truth. The clerk eyed the paper, then the earnest faces of the three young men. He sighed, the weight of the late hour and their apparent desperation softening his stance.

"Alright, follow me. We've got a few spares in the back."

He led them into the storage room where they

kept the extra phones. "I shouldn't be doing this. These are expensive pieces of modern technology and I don't understand why anyone would want to take them apart."

"I assure you," Matthew remarked casually, "they're going for a good cause."

As they followed the clerk into the room, Edwin couldn't resist another jab at Tom. "Let's hope the kid doesn't break anything while we're here."

Tom shot him a glare. "I'm more than capable of handling delicate equipment, Bancroft. Just worry about yourself."

One by one, the clerk reached up and removed three fully assembled telephones, placing them on the counter. "Here you are." Just as they started to reach across the counter he grabbed them and pulled them back. "Wait a minute. Are you wanting to take these phones apart so you can steal their designs and sell them yourselves?"

Matthew was just about to hand over the cash when the clerk made this accusation. He was at a sudden loss for words. That wasn't what they planned to use them for but how could he prove otherwise? "I..."

Suddenly, Edwin reached over and grabbed some extra money from Matthew's hand and waved it at the clerk as he asked, "Does it matter?"

The telephone operator immediately pocketed the extra money and told them to enjoy their new phones.

Leaving the telegraph office, the trio made their way back through the streets. The rivalry between Tom and Edwin continued to simmer, but the urgency of their mission kept them focused. They stopped at a few other shops along the way and picked up most of the other items on the lists.

By the time the three young men returned, Jedidiah, Phineas, and Myra had the basic frameworks ready. The additional parts from the phones allowed them to refine their design further.

Working quickly and efficiently, they constructed makeshift antennas and began assembling the communicators. They used batteries and hand cranks from the telephones to power the transmitters, incorporating a set of gears and cogs to turn the generator, providing it with the necessary power.

Jedidiah focused on the transmitters, Phineas on the receivers, and Myra coordinated their efforts, ensuring everything came together smoothly.

With their combined expertise, they managed to create a rudimentary wireless communication system. The final step was to test it. Initially, they tested it from just a few feet away.

"Okay, cross your fingers," Jedidiah said, holding up a makeshift microphone. "Matthew, can you hear me?"

A crackling sound came through the speaker,

followed by Matthew's voice. "Loud and clear, Jed! This is amazing!"

"We did it," Jedidiah said, wiping sweat from his brow. "Now, let's see if they work from further away."

They quickly installed the devices on their respective airships and tested the connection.

"Swift to Icarus, do you read?" Jedidiah called out.

There was a moment of static before Phineas' voice crackled through. "Icarus here, loud and clear."

"Enigma, do you read?" Jedidiah tried next.

Myra's voice came through, filled with excitement. "Enigma here, reading you loud and clear."

They all shouted with excitement; their new wireless communication system was a resounding success. They had created a way to communicate between their airships, giving them a significant advantage in the race.

"We'll need to fine-tune it and make improvements later," Phineas said, his eyes sparkling with excitement. "But this is a great start."

Myra nodded in agreement. "We'll continue to work together. This could revolutionize airship communication."

Jedidiah felt a surge of pride and determination.

They had overcome another challenge and were ready to face whatever lay ahead. "Let's get back in the air and catch up with the others. Paris is waiting for us."

The three airships lifted off, their crews now connected by wireless communication. The sky was the limit, and they were ready to soar.

As they flew through the night, the excitement of their recent success and the anticipation of the next leg of their journey filled the air. Jedidiah, at the helm of the Swift, adjusted their course, ensuring they maintained a steady speed of thirty-two knots. The dark expanse of the sky was dotted with stars, providing a serene backdrop for their trip. The gentle hum of the engines provided a comforting soundtrack.

Matthew joined Jedidiah on the deck, a thoughtful expression on his face. "It's amazing how quickly we managed to put together those wireless communicators," he said, his voice filled with admiration.

Jedidiah nodded, a smile playing on his lips. "It just shows you can do anything if you put your mind to it."

Their collaborative invention was already proving invaluable. Phineas' voice crackled through the receiver, his tone filled with excitement. "Icarus to Swift, we're maintaining our course and speed. Everything is running smoothly on our end."

"Good to hear, Phineas," Jedidiah replied. "Let's keep up the good work. Paris is just a few hours away."

Meanwhile, on the Enigma, Myra and Edwin were also feeling the exhilaration of their recent success. Myra adjusted the controls, her eyes focused on the horizon. "We've come a long way, Edwin," she said, a hint of pride in her voice.

Her nephew nodded, his earlier shame replaced by determination. "We'll win this race, Aunt Myra. I promise."

In the early hours of the next morning, Jedidiah, at the helm of the Swift, noticed a sudden change in the weather. He called to his childhood friend sleeping in the cabin behind him, "Matt, wake up! The weather's getting rough," his voice was tense. "We need to prepare for turbulence."

Phineas' voice crackled through the receiver. "Icarus to Swift. Icarus to Enigma. We're about to fly directly into a huge storm front."

"Any way to fly around it?" Myra's voice crackled through the loudspeaker.

"No," Phineas replied firmly. "It looks too extensive to navigate around. We'll have to go through it. Everyone, secure your equipment and prepare for rough skies."

The three captains relayed the message to their crews. Tension filled the air as they approached the ominous clouds. The first gusts of wind hit the airships, causing them to sway. Lightning flashed in the distance, illuminating the dark clouds with an eerie glow.

"Hold steady!" Jedidiah called out, gripping the helm tightly. The Swift shuddered as it was buffeted by strong winds. Rain began to pour down in sheets, reducing visibility to almost nothing.

On the Enigma, Myra and Edwin worked together to keep their airship steady. "Stay focused, Edwin!" Myra shouted over the howling wind. "We've trained for this. We can handle it."

Edwin nodded, his hands gripping the controls tightly. "I'm with you, Aunt Myra. We won't let this storm beat us."

Meanwhile, aboard the Icarus, Phineas and Tom struggled against the violent winds. "Keep the engines running at full power!" Phineas ordered. "We need all the thrust we can get to stay on course."

Tom, drenched by the rain, worked tirelessly to maintain the engine's performance.

For hours, the airships battled the storm. Communication between them was sporadic, the static-filled transmissions barely audible over the roar of the wind and thunder. The crews worked tirelessly, their determination unwavering despite the relentless weather. There were times when the reception was so bad they couldn't hear each other at all.

Suddenly, a blinding flash of lightning tore through the sky, followed by a deafening crack of thunder. The bolt appeared to directly target the Enigma, illuminating its frame in a ghostly white glow.

Lightening tore through
the sky, targeting the Enigma.

CHAPTER XVIII

Arrival in Paris

"Myra!" Phineas shouted from the deck of the Icarus, lunging forward in panic while Tom grabbed the microphone and desperately tried to contact the Enigma. Simultaneously, he attempted to reach out to the Swift but received no response from either. The electric discharge from the lightning strike had shorted out the communication devices on all three ships.

As the storm raged around them, the crew of the Icarus anxiously peered into the churning darkness. Just then, a small break in the storm clouds offered a moment of clarity. To everyone's immense relief, the Enigma emerged through the rain, its silhouette gradually becoming visible again. Remarkably, it appeared completely unharmed. The lightning hadn't fazed it. Everyone aboard the other two vessels celebrated as they breathed a sigh of relief. However, their trouble wasn't over just yet.

For the next couple of hours, the crews battled the relentless storm. They tightened their grip on the controls and focused intently on securing their equipment. Navigation became a test of endurance and skill as they cautiously maneuvered through the turbulent skies. The wind howled ferociously, and sheets of rain battered against the airships, but their determination never wavered. With each passing minute, they drew closer to their destination, resilient in the face of nature's fury.

Finally, as dawn approached, the storm began to subside. The dark clouds gave way to the soft light of the rising sun, casting a golden glow over the drenched airships. The exhausted crews breathed a collective sigh of relief. Jedidiah turned to Matthew and said, "We made it through!"

At approximately 6:36 AM local time, Paris came into view. The sprawling city filled the crews with a sense of accomplishment. They had made it to another checkpoint.

Jedidiah, Phineas, and Myra guided their airships toward the designated landing area within walking distance of the Palais de l'Industrie, their hearts filled with anticipation. As they descended, the sound of cheering spectators reached their ears. Jedidiah's attention was quickly drawn to the sight of the other three airships, the Valkyrie, the Albatross, and the Dauntless, still grounded due to the storm. The unexpected advantage filled him with renewed determination.

"Looks like that storm was good luck for us after all!" Jedidiah pointed ecstatically toward their competitors' vessels.

"We still have a chance!" Matthew shouted as he scooped up the semaphore flags and signaled the other ships. Phineas and Myra shared his enthusiasm.

Once on the ground, the crews quickly disembarked, their eyes scanning the crowd for the checkpoint officials. They were eager to collect their next falcon statue and continue their journey.

The official at the Paris checkpoint greeted them warmly, handing each of them a bronze miniature falcon, the third statue and fourth token of their journey. "Congratulations on making it to Paris," the official said, his voice filled with genuine admiration. "You're now one step closer to the final destination."

Jedidiah accepted his statue, a determined look in his eyes. "Thank you. I think I can speak for everyone when I say we're all more than ready for the final leg of this race."

The official nodded, then gestured towards a nearby tent where several large barrels full of coal were stacked. "You'll need to refuel for the journey ahead. Our supply team will assist you. Please follow me."

The three airship captains followed him to the

tent, where several workers were busy preparing the fuel. The official turned back to the group and explained, "You'll be given enough coal for your steam engines to reach Wichita, but you'll need to plan your route carefully to ensure you don't run out. It's a long journey, and conditions can be unpredictable."

Phineas glanced at the barrels and then back at the official. "Do we have any options for additional fuel stops along the way?"

The official nodded. "You'll be able to make a brief rest stop in New York and replenish your supply if you choose. However, our coal is of the highest quality and should last you from here to there."

Myra stepped forward, her expression determined. "We'll make it work. We've come this far, and we're not about to give up now."

The official smiled. "That's the spirit. Once you're restocked, you'll be ready to continue your journey. However, like your competitors, we advise you to wait a few hours before taking off. We're expecting rolling storm fronts throughout the morning."

Taking this advice to heart, the crews of the Swift, the Icarus, and the Enigma quickly set to work, loading the barrels onto their airships and checking their equipment one last time. The atmosphere was charged with a mix of excitement and tension as they prepared for the longest leg of the race yet. Phineas B. Hargroves suggested that while they had time, they should make some repairs and upgrades to their communication system.

The three captains immediately set to work on this project. However, they quickly realized they needed more metal to complete the necessary upgrades and boost their signal.

"We need copper to get this done right," Phineas said, frustration evident in his voice. "Without it, we won't have the range we need."

"We can also use it to ground them, so they don't short out again." Myra quickly added.

A realization suddenly struck Phineas. "So that's how the lightning had such little effect on your ship. You turned the entire vessel into a lightning rod."

Myra smiled as she nodded her head. "You catch on fast."

An official passing by overheard their discussion and approached them. "You might find what you're looking for on Rue de Chazelles. It used to be a foundry, but it's currently being used as a workshop. They have the largest supply of copper in all of France, but I'm not sure if they'll sell any of it. They're using it for an enormous project."

Jedidiah nodded. "Thanks for the tip. We'll head over there now."

This time, Phineas, Jedidiah, and Myra decided to go on the scavenger hunt, leaving Matthew, Tom, and Edwin behind to guard the ships. They set off through the bustling streets of Paris.

By the time they reached the workshop on Rue de Chazelles, the skies had opened up, and rain poured down in torrents. They hurried to the entrance, their clothes drenched and clinging to them. Phineas knocked on the heavy wooden door, and after a moment, it creaked open to reveal a burly man with a skeptical expression.

"What do you want?" he asked gruffly, eyeing them warily.

"We're in desperate need of copper for our communication devices," Jedidiah explained quickly. "We've heard you have the largest supply in France, and we're willing to pay for it."

The man hesitated, glancing back into the workshop. "Maybe you haven't heard, but we're working on a pretty important project here. We need every single ounce of this copper."

Myra stepped forward, her eyes pleading. "Please, it's crucial for our journey. We won't need much, just enough to boost our signal and ground our systems."

After a tense silence, another man stepped up and dismissed the first one. He turned to the three visitors and said, "Please come in, I'll see what I can do."

"Thank you, Mr...?"

"Eiffel," the man smiled through his well-trimmed beard. "Gustave Eiffel, but you can just call me Gustave."

They were led further into the workshop, the space filled with the hum of activity as workers toiled over various components for an enormous statue. The sound of hammers striking metal echoed through the cavernous room, mingling with the patter of rain on the roof. They were directed to a corner where large sheets of copper were stacked.

"Take what you need, but be quick about it," the man instructed. "And don't forget, you're interrupting important work here."

"Thank you," Phineas said gratefully as he walked past the sheets and picked up a few buckets of scrap copper sitting on the floor. "We don't need a full sheet. This will do nicely."

Outside, the storm intensified, thunder rumbling ominously in the distance. They had no choice but to wait there.

That's when they spotted it: the head and shoulders of the largest statue any of them had ever seen. Not too far from it, stashed in another section of the workshop, was a giant arm holding a tremendous torch.

"Egads!" Phineas exclaimed. "Is that what I think it is?"

"The people of France's gift to America?"

Looming before them were the
head and shoulders of the largest
statue they had ever seen.

Gustave smiled proudly. "It is indeed. Although, as you can see, it's still a few years away from completion."

Jedidiah, Phineas, and Myra had read about the statue and even seen stereoscopic images of its torch-bearing arm during its brief display in Philadelphia back in 1876. The three airship captains gathered for a closer look at the shiny copper structures.

****

Meanwhile, back at the landing field, Matthew, Tom, and Edwin had taken refuge from the storm aboard the Swift. The confined space and the tension between Tom and Edwin were still thick. Edwin couldn't resist another jab as he observed Tom studying the dismantled communication device by the helm.

"Try not to get any of the parts sticky," Edwin sneered. "I know how you kids like your peppermint sticks, licorice, and other candies."

Tom, who had silently endured Edwin's taunts for far too long, finally snapped. "I've had enough of your snide remarks, Bancroft!" he shouted, shoving Edwin back. "Maybe it's time you stopped acting like a spoiled brat."

Edwin, not one to back down, pushed back, and the two young men began to scuffle. Matthew, who had been trying to keep the peace, initially stepped in to break up the fight. But then, an idea struck him.

"That's enough!" Matthew yelled, forcing himself between them. "This feud has to end, and if fighting is the only way to settle it, then so be it. But it will be a fair fight, with rules, and I'll referee."

Both Tom and Edwin looked at him, breathing heavily but nodding in agreement. Matthew cleared some space in Jedidiah's sleeping cabin, moved the two cots, and threw the mattress on the floor. After that, he set the terms.

"This will be a civil match, no dirty tricks. The first to yield or be unable to continue loses. Agreed?"

"Agreed," they both replied, though still glaring at each other. They each kicked off their shoes and stepped onto the mattresses.

On the count of three, the match began, initially a clash of strength and will. Tom and Edwin circled each other, throwing punches and vying for the upper hand. Matthew kept a close eye, ready to intervene if necessary.

As the fight wore on, it became clear that both young men were evenly matched. They grappled and exchanged blows, but neither could maintain dominance for long. Their determination to settle their differences fueled their stamina, but exhaustion was inevitable.

Finally, after what felt like an eternity, both Tom and Edwin collapsed onto the floor, panting. Tom, using the last of his strength, managed to stand and extend a hand to Edwin.

"Truce?" Tom asked, breathing heavily.

Edwin, lying on the floor, looked up at Tom's outstretched hand. A slow smile spread across his face as he accepted it, allowing himself to be pulled to his feet. "Truce."

They both started laughing, the tension between them dissipating as they realized how ridiculous their rivalry had been. Matthew smiled, relieved that the feud was finally over.

"You both fought well," Colton remarked. "Now let's put this behind us and focus on winning the race."

Tom and Edwin nodded, their mutual respect renewed. They shook hands once more. "You're okay, kid..." Edwin stopped and corrected himself, "Tom. You're okay, Tom!"

"Thanks, Bancroft..." Tom replied, smiling. "I mean, Edwin."

****

As the storm began to slack off once more, the skies slowly lightened, and the rain lessened to a drizzle. The atmosphere inside the Swift was more relaxed, and the tension between Tom and Edwin was finally resolved.

Outside, the crews of the other airships took advantage of the brief lull in the storm to finish their repairs and preparations. The sky, although still overcast, no longer seemed as menacing. The sound of hammering and the clanking of tools filled the air as everyone worked diligently.

Unknown to any of them, hovering just outside the city, a mysterious and ominous airship loomed. Its dark, sleek design contrasted sharply with the lighter, more traditional airships grounded below.

Standing alone at the helm of this foreboding vessel was Jonathan Blake. With his mask firmly in place, he looked through a long, brass telescope and surveyed the scene before him. He could see all six of the grounded airships and their crews.

Beneath his mask, Blake's lips curled into a sinister smile as he observed the chaos and urgency below. His eyes gleamed with malevolent satisfaction.

CHAPTER XIX

The Final Revelation

As the storm continued to slacken, Jedidiah Davenport, Phineas B. Hargroves, and Myra Wilhelmina Bancroft left the workshop, their spirits lifted despite the steady rain. Gustave Eiffel had been more accommodating than they could have hoped, and now they carried the crucial copper needed to upgrade their communication systems.

"We need to get these upgrades done quickly," Jedidiah said, his voice tinged with urgency. "Every minute counts now."

Phineas nodded, his expression determined. "We've come this far, and we can't afford any more delays. Let's get back and make sure our communication systems are fully functioning before we take off."

Myra, always the pragmatist, added, "And let's not forget to check everything else. We have a long journey ahead before our one and only rest stop."

As they approached the landing field, the familiar shapes of the Swift, the Icarus, and the Enigma came into view as well as the other three ships.

Matthew, Tom, and Edwin had already begun making some final inspections. The tension from earlier was completely gone and replaced by a shared focus on the task at hand.

"Did you get it?" Matthew called out as they approached.

"Yes, and more than enough," Phineas replied, holding up the buckets of copper. "Let's get to work."

The teams quickly split up, each member falling into a well-practiced routine. Jedidiah, Phineas, and Myra set to work on the communication devices, carefully incorporating the copper to enhance their signal strength.

"What do you think?" Jedidiah asked, glancing up from the wooden box filled with mechanical parts.

"We're making good progress," Phineas said, fastening a connection into place. "This should give us the range we need."

Myra nodded in agreement. "Just a little more, and we'll be ready."

As they worked, the storm outside continued to subside, the dark clouds temporarily giving way to patches of blue sky. The brief respite in the weather brought a sense of calm, but the urgency of their mission kept them focused.

Finally, after what felt like hours but was only a short while, the upgrades were complete. Jedidiah tested the system, and the clear, strong signal brought smiles to their faces.

"We did it," he said, satisfaction evident in his voice. "Now we can keep in touch no matter what happens."

"Good," Myra said, wiping her hands. "Let's finish up and get ready to take off. We don't want to fall behind again."

"Precisely," Phineas agreed. "This storm has guaranteed us an even start with the other racers."

Suddenly, a commotion erupted outside. All six of them hurried to see what was happening, only to find Sir Reginald Fortescue and Captain Jonathan Braddock confronting the two men they had each hired as their crewmates. Both had been caught tampering with the engines of their ships, the Albatross and the Valkyrie.

"Briggs! What the devil do you think you're doing?" Sir Reginald shouted, his face red with anger.

"And you, Carter! I never want you stepping foot on my ship again!" Braddock bellowed, his fists clenched in rage.

Officials quickly rushed over as the two men screamed for help. "We've caught the saboteurs!"

They shouted.

The officials moved quickly to detain Briggs and Carter while the crowd buzzed with excitement.

Suddenly realizing that Professor Montgomery had also hired his crewmate from the same place they acquired theirs, they began calling for him to come out.

Professor Thaddeus Montgomery reluctantly exited his ship, the Dauntless, with his hired man Dawson in tow. As soon as Phineas and Myra saw him, their faces paled. They each immediately recognized him!

"That's the scoundrel who attacked me on Founders' Day in Spoon Fork!" Phineas shouted in anger.

Jedidiah's eyes narrowed as he recognized Dawson as well. "And he's the one who I saw running out of your hotel room in Wichita," he added, his tone cold and filled with resolve.

"You're all under arrest for sabotage," one official declared. But just as one of the men started to move towards Dawson, something unexpected happened that took them all by surprise. Both he and Professor Thaddeus Montgomery pulled out revolvers and aimed them at the crowd.

"I don't think so!" Montgomery shouted as he and the other three men raced aboard the Dauntless.

Still hovering overhead, Jonathan Blake

witnessed the entire incident through his telescope. He moved his ship closer, suddenly aiming his ultrasonic disruptor cannon at the mass of people, including the officials. As the sonic waves emanated from the cannon, the effect was immediate and devastating. People began clutching their heads, faces contorted in agony. Some dropped to their knees, disoriented and incapacitated. Others staggered and fell to the ground, rendered helpless by the invisible assault. This provided Professor Montgomery and the other three men ample time to make their escape.

Amidst the chaos, Phineas and Myra, though terribly disoriented, managed to look towards the ship. Through their blurred vision and the haze of pain, they spotted their old friend Jonathan Blake at the helm. Despite the fact that he was still wearing his disguise, they knew it was him. Their eyes widened in shock and disbelief as the realization sank in.

"Jonathan!" the two eccentric older airship captains shouted in unison.

Blake continued to hold everyone at bay while the Dauntless took off, its steam engine roaring to life as it ascended into the sky. Just as it vanished from sight, Blake's cannon suddenly powered down, losing pressure and ceasing its assault. This provided everyone time to recover.

Jedidiah winced as he stood up and quickly

assessed the situation. "We need to get to the Swift," he said urgently. "It's the only one equipped with a cannon. It'll be our only chance to take out Blake."

The group nodded in agreement, their determination renewed despite the lingering effects of the sonic attack. They sprinted toward the Swift, the airship that now held their last hope of turning the tide against their formidable foe.

As they boarded the ship, the sky began to darken again as the weather took a final turn for the worse. Jedidiah quickly took the helm. Phineas and Myra manned the controls of the disruptor cannon, while Matthew, Tom, and Edwin secured the rest of the equipment. The engines roared to life, and the Swift began to ascend rapidly.

Unfortunately, as they reached the sky, they realized they would be battling not only Blake but also the storm, which was quickly intensifying. Dark clouds rolled in rapidly, and the wind began to howl as the storm resumed its full fury.

Blake, seeing the Swift take flight, worked quickly to reactivate his weapon. Aiming at the airship, he unleashed another devastating blast. The sound waves rippled through the air, heading straight for them, cutting through the torrential rain and gusting winds.

"He's targeting us!" Tom shouted, his voice barely audible over the howling storm.

"Hold steady," Jedidiah commanded his hands firm on the controls despite the ship being buffeted by the fierce winds. "Phineas, Myra, get ready to fire back."

They worked quickly, adjusting the settings on their cannon to counter Blake's attack. The two airships faced each other in the stormy skies, the tension strong, with lightning illuminating the dark clouds around them.

"Now!" Jedidiah yelled.

Phineas and Myra fired the Swift's disruptor cannon, the powerful blast meeting Blake's attack head-on. The two sonic waves collided in mid-air, creating a visible shockwave that reverberated through the stormy clouds.

Blake's airship shuddered from the impact, but he remained resolute, preparing for another strike. The Swift, bolstered by the determination of its crew, held its ground against both him and the battering storm.

"Prepare for another shot!" Jedidiah ordered. "We can't let him get the upper hand."

As the Swift maneuvered for a better position, Blake adjusted his aim, readying his cannon for another blast. The skies around them crackled with tension, thunder booming in the distance, the outcome of this aerial duel hanging in the balance.

Determined to take them down once and for all, Blake adjusted the controls to his ship and ascended higher into the sky, seeking a better vantage point. As he adjusted his aim, a sudden flash of lightning struck his airship. The airbag burst into flames, rapidly disintegrating and leaving the vessel in a fiery inferno.

"Myra, look!" Phineas shouted in terror, pointing at Blake's ship engulfed in flames.

Myra's eyes widened as she saw her old friend climbing over the railing and leaping off, trying to escape the blaze. Without hesitation, she grabbed the rope attached to the large pulley from above the cargo hold, tied it around her waist, and leaped over the railing of the Swift as Blake fell past. She caught him in mid-air, and they free-fell a short distance before the rope suddenly stopped them.

Everyone rushed to the side of the ship and breathed a sigh of relief to see the two of them unharmed. However, it was at this moment that Phineas B. Hargroves noticed the rope fraying under their weight. Thinking quickly, he grabbed one of the leather packs he had given Jedidiah before they left for the trip. They were sitting on the deck next to the railing. Everyone gasped as he leaped over the side of the Swift as well. Phineas descended rapidly toward Myra and Blake, reaching them just as the rope snapped.

The three clung to each other as they began plummeting toward the earth, rain whipping against their faces. With one swift motion, Phineas pulled

Lightning struck his airship causing
the airbag to burst into flames.

the cord on the pack, releasing a silk parachute of his design. The sudden jerk slowed their fall, but the descent remained turbulent, buffeted by the storm's fierce winds. They struggled to maintain their grip as they were tossed about by a series of jolts and sways before reaching the ground.

On the Swift, everyone breathed another collective sigh of relief as they watched the trio land safely. However, Jedidiah's expression changed to one of alarm as he realized Blake's ship was now a massive ball of fire directly above them and descending rapidly.

"We need to move, now!" Jedidiah shouted, his hands flying over the controls as the storm raged on.

He piloted the Swift away from the impending danger, the engines roaring as the airship maneuvered to safety. As they landed away from the inferno, the crew quickly disembarked.

Myra, Phineas, and Blake touched down on the ground, the parachute billowing wildly around them. They turned and watched the remains of the airship landing in the Seine River. Fortunately, all spectators had managed to move safely out of the way.

Jedidiah, Matthew, Tom, and Edwin rushed over to them and helped Phineas out of his harness. As soon as he was free, they all ran back to the Swift to get out of the pouring rain. Once they were on board, they went down into the cargo hold, shook off the water, and caught their breath.

"Are you all alright?" they asked, concern etched on their faces.

"We're fine," Phineas replied, his voice steady.

Blake, shaken but unharmed, removed the plague mask he had worn as a disguise and nodded in agreement. "Thank you," he said quietly to Myra and Phineas. "You saved my life."

"We couldn't just let you fall," Myra said, her voice gentle but firm.

Phineas smiled and said, "It's what friends do!"

"But I tried to kill both of you!"

"So," Phineas tried to make a joke out of the situation, "Everyone's entitled to a mistake." After a brief chuckle, he asked his old friend, "Why, Jonathan? Why did you do it? Why did you never tell us you were alive?"

"Revenge," Blake replied simply.

"So you did blame us for the accident?" Myra asked.

Jonathan Blake shrugged and said, "Wouldn't you?" He turned and looked off into the distance as the rain continued to pour outside, recalling that fateful event twenty years ago.

****

The memory of that day was still vivid for

Jonathan Blake. He had been with Phineas and Myra on that expedition in the mountains, always the mediator, trying to keep the peace between his two competitive friends. Most of what he remembered aligned with their version of events.

As they were ascending to the top of the mountain, Jonathan had tried to keep them cautious. "We should slow down," he had said, his breath visible in the cold air. "The snow looks unstable. We need to be careful."

But Phineas had laughed, waving off Jonathan's concerns. "We'll be fine, old friend. Just a bit further, and we'll reach the summit."

Myra had smirked, her competitive spirit flaring. "Don't tell me you're afraid of a little snow, Jonathan."

Ignoring his advice, Phineas and Myra pressed on, their rivalry blinding them to the danger. The snow beneath their feet had crunched with every step, a subtle warning they failed to heed. Jonathan had followed closely, his eyes scanning the slope for any signs of trouble.

Suddenly, the ground beneath them had begun to shift. A deep rumble echoed through the mountains, and the snow started to slide. In their haste, Phineas and Myra had triggered an avalanche.

"Run!" Jonathan had shouted, his voice filled with panic.

Phineas and Myra had turned, their faces pale with fear. The roaring wave of snow and ice was upon them in seconds. Jonathan had pushed them both forward, trying to get them to safety. But the avalanche had been too fast, too powerful.

Jonathan had been caught in the middle, swept away by the unstoppable force. The snow and ice had engulfed him, pulling him under and knocking him unconscious.

When Jonathan had finally come to, he found himself buried deep beneath the snow. Disoriented and struggling to breathe, he had clawed his way to the surface. His head throbbed, and his vision was blurred, but he was alive. However, the impact had caused him to lose his memory. He couldn't recall who he was or how he had ended up in the mountains.

For months, Jonathan had wandered, surviving in the wilderness until he was found by a group of mountaineers. They had taken him to a nearby village, where he slowly began to recover. The villagers had been kind, helping him piece together fragments of his past. Bit by bit, his memory had started to return, but it took years for him to fully regain his sense of self.

By the time Jonathan had made his way back to London, Phineas and Myra had already moved on, both becoming celebrated inventors, scientists, and airship captains. The sight of their success had filled him with a deep-seated rage. He blamed them not only for the accident but for not conducting a thorough enough search for him, for giving up on him and assuming he was dead.

Jonathan's resentment had festered, turning into a burning desire for revenge. He had spent years planning the perfect way to make them pay for what they had done, using his skills and knowledge to sabotage their work and undermine their success at every turn.

****

"I lied, cheated, and stole from everyone just to get what I wanted," Blake stated with great remorse. "I wasn't as smart as the two of you, so the only way to get the inventions I needed to plot my revenge was to take them from others. After laying low for a while, I realized I needed a base of operations where I could stay under the radar. I eventually opened a little shop in Toronto, a city bustling with innovation and far from where anyone would recognize me."

"On Automaton Alley?" Jedidiah suddenly spoke up from the sidelines.

Jonathan nodded. "How'd you know?"

"I met your... employees," the young entrepreneur replied casually. "And I found a number of my own blueprints in your shop."

"Oh yes, Artemis and Apollo," Jonathan smiled. "The only things I ever designed myself, and both were based on other people's work. I've never created anything completely original in my life."

"Oh, I don't know about that," Myra replied mysteriously.

Jonathan continued, "After setting up shop, I realized I needed some muscle and expertise to carry out my plans. That's when I crossed paths with Briggs, Dawson, Carter, and Professor Thaddeus Montgomery. All four of them had bounties out for their arrest across America. They were infamous in their own rights. Briggs was a notorious gunslinger, Dawson a skilled saboteur, Carter a master thief, and Montgomery a rogue scientist."

Jedidiah raised an eyebrow. "Quite the motley crew you assembled there, Mr. Blake," he remarked, his voice barely rising above the sound of the rain pounding against the side of the ship.

Jonathan shrugged. "Desperate times called for desperate measures. They had taken refuge in Canada to escape their bounties in the US. They were willing to work for me for a cut of the prize money when the Dauntless won the race."

"The Dauntless!" Edwin Bancroft exclaimed, raising his voice over a clap of thunder. "So you never intended to let the Enigma win, did you?"

"Of course not," Blake admitted. "The plan was

to make it look like each ship was being sabotaged, including Montgomery's ship. That way, when he won, it wouldn't look obvious that it had been rigged. Dawson, Briggs, and Carter each took on the roles of crewmates aboard the Dauntless, the Albatross, and the Valkyrie."

Jonathan sighed as he continued. "As part of the alliance we formed, I agreed to place some high-wager bets on their behalf. The Dauntless was guaranteed to win." Blake turned back to his old friends and asked, "Can the two of you ever forgive me?"

Phineas and Myra exchanged glances, their faces softening with compassion.

"Jonathan," Phineas began, stepping forward and placing a hand on his old friend's shoulder, "consider the matter forgotten."

Myra nodded with understanding. "We can't change the past, but we can start anew."

Blake's face lit up as he felt the weight of decades lifting from his shoulders. "Thank you."

Myra smiled gently, but then her expression grew serious. "Jonathan, are you sure you've recovered all your memories from before the accident?"

Jonathan looked confused, his brow furrowing. "What do you mean?"

Myra took a deep breath, motioning for her nephew, to come closer. He stepped forward hesitantly.

"There's no easy way to say this other than to just come right out," Myra said, her voice steady but her eyes searching Jonathan's face. "Jonathan Blake, meet your son, Edwin Bancroft."

CHAPTER XX

Race to the Finish

"His what?" Edwin Bancroft whirled his head and looked at his aunt in disbelief.

Myra Wilhelmina Bancroft smiled as she said, "Edwin, this is your father, Jonathan Blake." Everyone gasped upon hearing this sudden revelation.

Jonathan looked at the young man more closely, suddenly beginning to see the resemblance. "This is mine and Rebecca's son?"

The eccentric older woman nodded, glad to see he was beginning to remember. "He was born about eight months after we thought you had... well, after the accident."

Jonathan Blake was at a complete and total loss for words, and so was his son. The revelation of Edwin's parentage left everyone stunned, but there was little time to dwell on it. The race was far from over, and all four criminals were still out there.

"Well, now that everything has been settled," Phineas declared, his voice steady and determined, "we need to get back in the air and finish this race. We've come too far to let those scoundrels steal the victory."

They all made their way out of the cargo hold and back onto the deck. Phineas looked up at the clearing sky. "I think the storms are finally over."

Jonathan, now reintegrated with his old friends and son, nodded in agreement. "I'll help in any way I can."

Suddenly, Jedidiah stepped up with an air of authority. "I agree, we need to get back out there, but first we need to make this a fair race." He turned on his heel and started toward the Albatross and the Valkyrie. "What say we all work together and help Sir Reginald Fortescue and Captain Braddock get their engines repaired?" Everyone unanimously agreed. They divided into two teams and offered their assistance to their fellow competitors, both of whom thankfully accepted.

With clear blue skies above them, all remaining ships were finally ready for takeoff. Jedidiah Davenport and Matthew Colton took their places on the Swift. Phineas B. Hargroves and Tom Miller manned their stations on the Icarus. Myra Wilhelmina Bancroft, Edwin Bancroft, and Jonathan Blake boarded the Enigma. Sir Reginald Fortescue and Captain Braddock remained on board their own vessels. The engines of each ship roared to life, and they all ascended into the air.

As they flew over the French countryside, the Swift's improved communication system crackled to life. "Swift to Icarus, Swift to Enigma, do you read?" Jedidiah called out.

"Loud and clear," Phineas replied, relief evident in his voice.

"Same here," Myra added. "We're right behind you, Swift."

"Keep an eye out for the Dauntless," Jedidiah instructed, his eyes scanning the horizon. "If we see them, maybe we can help bring them to justice."

With their course set for Wichita, the finish line of the race, the airships soared through the noonday sky, each crew pushing their vessels but keeping a steady pace. The tension was intense, everyone realizing their journey would soon be coming to an end.

Around eight o'clock that night, they all started soaring high above the Atlantic Ocean, leaving land behind once again. This time, they would be flying over the sea for almost four days straight.

The vastness of the ocean beneath them was both awe-inspiring and daunting. The crews remained vigilant, their eyes trained on the horizon and the gauges of their airships. Every now and then, the communication lines would crackle with brief updates, maintaining their coordinated formation.

"Steady as she goes," Jedidiah muttered to himself, adjusting the controls of the Swift.

Phineas' voice crackled over the radio. "We should reach the American coast by Thursday morning if we keep this pace."

"Roger that," Myra responded. "How's everyone holding up?"

"Tired but determined," Matthew replied, echoing the sentiment of all the crews.

As the days passed, the airships cut through the skies, their engines humming steadily. The sense of competition was ever-present, but so was a newfound camaraderie. After all, they had shared the highs and lows of this extraordinary journey, and now, they were closing in on the final stretch together.

On Thursday morning, September 15th, 1881, the coastline of the United States came into view. Cheers erupted over the radios as the crews celebrated the sight of land after days of endless ocean.

"Land ho!," Jedidiah announced excitedly over the communication system.

All five airships hovered over the bustling city of New York. The crews of each vessel faced a crucial decision: whether to land and replenish their fuel supplies, ensuring they had enough to reach Wichita without risking running out over the vast

Midwest.

The Swift, the Icarus, and the Enigma, after precise calculations, determined they had enough coal to make it to the finish and chose to push on, relying on their meticulous planning and careful navigation.

Captain Braddock's Valkyrie and Sir Reginald Fortescue's Albatross, however, opted to land in New York. The risk of running out of fuel was too great for them, and they didn't want to jeopardize their chances in the final leg of the race. They touched down briefly, hiring men to swiftly load new barrels of coal onto their ships. Within a short amount of time, they were back in the air, trailing after the others.

That night was particularly cloudy, and the stars were nowhere to be seen. Each crew had to rely strictly on their navigation equipment to steer by. Jedidiah stayed up most of the night steering the Swift, while Matthew slept in the cabin. A couple of hours before sunrise, his childhood friend got up and offered to take over. Completely exhausted, Davenport agreed.

A few hours later, Jedidiah was awakened by the sounds of Matthew shouting, "Hey, you dunderheads! You're going the wrong way!"

The young entrepreneur leaped from his bed and joined him at the helm. "What's going on?" He shielded his eyes from the rising sun and squinted to see what Matthew was so upset about.

"It's the Albatross and the Valkyrie!" Matthew pointed at the two airships sailing straight toward them. "They're going the wrong way!"

"Going the wrong way?" Jedidiah repeated in disbelief. "That's ridiculous! How did they even get ahead of us?" Still shielding his eyes, it suddenly dawned on him and he glanced at his old friend. "Matt, what direction does the sun rise from?"

"The east," Matthew replied, not understanding why he was being asked this.

"And which direction is Wichita from New York?"

"West..." Matthew's eyes suddenly widened as realization hit him, seeing the two ships pass them going in the opposite direction. "Jed, I don't know how this could have happened. I was following the compass!"

Jedidiah glanced down and spotted a horseshoe lying next to the instrument. He picked it up, and the needle spun wildly. "Is this by any chance magnetic?"

"Yeah," Matthew explained. "Pat Bennington gave it to me before we left. Said it would bring us luck. He uses it to pick up loose nails and stuff."

Davenport covered his face with his hand and took a deep breath before saying, "Okay, so obviously you didn't know that magnets can disrupt a compass. It's fine. I'm sure we're not that far behind. Let's just turn this ship around and make up for lost time."

After maintaining a steady speed and taking a slightly different path for a few hours, the Swift finally came close enough to the Icarus and the Enigma to hear their broadcasts over the radio. They had been periodically calling out all day, trying to reach him.

"Swift, this is the Icarus... do you... us?" Phineas' voice crackled through the speakers, heavy with static.

Jedidiah quickly grabbed the microphone, relief flooding his voice. "Icarus, we read you... loud and clear... been off course... compass malfunction," he managed to say through the interference.

"Where... you been?... worried sick!" Myra's voice cut in and out, also distorted by the static.

Jedidiah explained the mix-up with the compass and how they had ended up off course. The radio continued to crackle, making it difficult to hear every word.

"We... would have... back... look for you, but... know at... point... separated... what course... might have taken," Phineas' voice came through, fragmented but understandable.

"Well... back together... let's push... Wichita... finish this...," Jedidiah said, determination clear despite the broken transmission.

The connection faded in and out, but it was

enough to convey their messages. The Swift continued pushing on to catch up with everyone else.

By the next day, thanks to some clever navigation on his part, Jedidiah could pick up the radio signals from the other ships with more clarity, as they were now only thirty minutes ahead of him. He learned that the Albatross and the Valkyrie had also managed to rejoin the Icarus and the Enigma. The Swift was the only one still trailing behind.

Later that evening, after pushing hard all day, they finally spotted the four ships in the distance. Using their special lens goggles, they confirmed it was the remaining contestants. The other airships were drawing dangerously close to Wichita and the finish line. Davenport estimated his friends were about an hour away from finishing the race.

"Almost there," Jedidiah said, his voice filled with anticipation. "We've made visual contact, so there's still hope!"

Just as Jedidiah was about to set the Swift on an intercept course, he and Matthew spotted the Dauntless, with the four outlaws aboard, traveling at an unusually slow speed.

"Why are they going so slow?" Matthew asked, confused.

"Probably trying to conserve fuel," Jedidiah replied simply. "They didn't stop for more in New York."

"Neither did we!" Matthew suddenly worried they wouldn't have enough coal to reach Wichita.

"Don't worry, I planned ours well," Jedidiah assured him as he banked hard on the wheel, his eyes narrowing. "I'm changing course. We're going after them!"

Matthew nodded as the Swift veered towards the Dauntless. The chase was brief, with the Swift's superior speed quickly closing the gap. The Dauntless, trying to conserve fuel, was no match for the determined crew of the Swift.

"Ready the ultrasonic disruptor cannon," Jedidiah commanded, his eyes fixed on the other ship.

Matthew quickly set the controls and, with precise aim, fired the cannon. The powerful waves rippled through the air, causing the Dauntless to shudder and falter. Unable to maintain altitude, it began to descend, forced to land in a clearing below.

Jedidiah and Matthew exchanged a triumphant glance. They had managed to ground their adversaries without a prolonged battle.

"Let's check on them," Jedidiah said, steering the Swift down and hovering at a safe distance.

As they drifted closer, Matthew stood ready to fire another blast from the cannon. Montgomery, Dawson, Briggs, and Carter were already scrambling down the loading ramp, trying to get away.

"You're out of fuel, aren't you?" Jedidiah shouted to them, his voice calm but firm.

Montgomery glared at them but didn't say a word; his facial expressions spoke volumes.

Matthew looked concerned. "What do we do with them, Jed? We can't leave them here."

Jedidiah thought for a moment. "They won't get very far on foot. We'll send the law back to get them later. Right now, we have a race to win."

As Davenport banked the Swift once again and set the course for the finish line, Matthew voiced his worries. "We'll never catch up now. The race is lost."

Jedidiah smiled, a twinkle of determination in his eye. "I wouldn't say that."

He turned a few knobs and adjusted several levers. The pressure in the steam engine began to rise, surpassing any levels Matthew had seen before.

"Hang on," Jedidiah said, gripping the controls.

With an intense push forward on the main lever, the Swift lurched from a cruising speed of 32 knots to a blazing 60 knots. The sudden acceleration caused them both to stumble backward, but they held on, the thrill of the chase reinvigorating them.

"Let's show them why I named this ship the Swift," Jedidiah shouted over the roar of the engines.

The airship sped through the skies, the landscape below blurring as they closed the distance between them and the other racers. The race was far from over, and with their newfound speed, victory was once again within their grasp.

Over the next thirty minutes, Jedidiah and Matthew felt the exhilaration of the chase as they rapidly started to gain on the other airships. The landscape whipped by beneath them as the Swift surged forward with an unprecedented burst of power. They quickly closed the gap, the distinctive shapes of the Enigma, the Valkyrie, the Icarus, and the Albatross growing larger with each passing minute.

"Myra's in the lead," Matthew called out, peering through his goggles with the special lenses. "Captain Braddock's right behind her, Phineas is in third, and Sir Reginald Fortescue is in fourth."

"Not for long," Jedidiah replied with a determined grin. He adjusted the controls, and the Swift responded with a powerful surge, easily overtaking Fortescue's Albatross.

They continued to push forward, the Swift's advanced steam engine performing admirably under the strain. Within minutes, they had passed Phineas's Icarus, then Captain Braddock's Valkyrie, leaving only Myra's Enigma ahead of them. Jedidiah focused intently, guiding the Swift ever closer to the finish line. The Enigma loomed large, and with one final burst of speed, they pulled alongside Myra's ship. The finish line was now in sight, the crowd below roaring in anticipation.

"Almost there!" Matthew shouted, excitement evident in his voice. Just as the Swift was about to overtake Myra, Jedidiah felt a sudden lurch as the airship began to slow. He checked the pressure gauges and realized he had allowed the coal supply to run dangerously low. His previous calculations didn't account for the extra mileage from their wrong direction or the brief encounter with the Dauntless.

"Quick, find some more coal!" he shouted.

Matthew Colton immediately sprang into action, frantically searching for more fuel. After a tense moment, he found one last small bucket of coal and quickly fed it into the steam engine. The additional fuel provided a much-needed boost. The Swift regained its speed, inching back ahead of the Enigma. Myra, realizing what was happening, pushed her own ship to the limit, but it wasn't enough.

The Swift crossed the finish line just moments ahead of the Enigma. The crowd erupted in cheers, their jubilation echoing across the airfield. Jedidiah Davenport had taken first place. Myra Wilhelmina Bancroft's Enigma took second place, with Captain Jonathan Braddock's Valkyrie coming in third. Phineas B. Hargroves' Icarus claimed fourth place, and Sir Reginald Fortescue's Albatross finished fifth.

Jedidiah and Matthew shouted triumphantly, their hearts pounding with the thrill of victory. They had done it. They had won the race. The sense of accomplishment was overwhelming, and as they used the last bit of fuel for propulsion, they descended to the ground where they were met with a hero's welcome.

The other crews gathered around, offering congratulations and handshakes. Myra, Phineas, and the others all expressed their admiration for the Swift's incredible performance.

"Well done, Jedidiah," Myra said, shaking his hand firmly. "You truly earned this victory."

Phineas clapped him on the back. "My dear boy, I knew you had something up your sleeve. That was some impressive flying. You must show me what type of modifications you did to your engine to produce that type of speed."

Sir Reginald and Captain Braddock nodded in agreement, their competitive spirits satisfied by the fair and thrilling race.

As the congratulations continued, Jedidiah and Matthew basked in the glow of their hard-fought victory. The journey had been long and challenging, but in the end, the Swift had lived up to its name, carrying them to a well-deserved win.

Still on board the Icarus, Edwin Bancroft stood

back, his disappointment evident. It wasn't because they hadn't come in first, but because he had lost the money to pay off his gambling debt and, ultimately, his Aunt's airship. At that moment, the man he had recently learned was his father stepped forward and held up the voucher for the debt owed against the Enigma. He smiled at Edwin and set it on fire with his lighter. Edwin was so thrilled, he threw his arms around his father and thanked him for what he had just done.

"Are you sure you can afford to do that after losing your own airship in that fire?" Edwin asked his father.

Jonathan Blake laughed heartily. "Oh, don't worry, it was fully insured, and for far more than it was worth!"

The two shared a joyful moment before joining the others in congratulating Jedidiah. Race officials pushed through the crowd, requesting to see the stamped case with the miniature falcons as proof of Jedidiah's journey. Upon inspection, they officially proclaimed him the winner and presented him with a full-size brass falcon statue with a copper top hat and steel monocle.

Jedidiah carefully set down the wooden box containing the miniatures and grunted as he lifted the nearly forty-pound statue into his arms. After briefly admiring it, he passed it to Matthew, who nearly dropped it, surprised by its weight.

The crowd erupted into cheers as Jedidiah
was officially proclaimed the winner.

Following this, Jedidiah was presented with a bank draft for one hundred thousand dollars. The crowd erupted into cheers.

"You did it, Jed!" Matthew shouted, still struggling to hold the brass statue. "You really did it!"

****

The next day at Davenport Ranch, the atmosphere was jubilant. Every one of his hired hands and many residents of Spoon Fork had gathered to celebrate Jedidiah's triumph and marvel at the statues—both miniature and full-size—he had brought back with him. It had been exactly two weeks since the race began, and the community was thrilled to have him home.

The ranch was adorned with colorful streamers and banners, while tables groaned under the weight of delicious food and drink. The focal point of the gathering was a large table displaying the impressive full-size brass falcon statue, complete with its copper top hat and steel monocle, alongside the wooden box containing the miniature falcons from each checkpoint.

Jedidiah stood proudly beside the display, his heart swelling with pride as he watched everyone admire the statues. Matthew stood by his side, sharing in the joy and reveling in the success of their remarkable journey.

Phineas, Tom, Myra, Edwin, and Jonathan mingled with the crowd, recounting stories from the race. Phineas animatedly explained the intricacies of the Icarus's engine to an attentive group, while Myra proudly introduced her nephew, Edwin, to everyone she saw.

Jonathan Blake, now fully embraced by the community, stood with a contented smile, grateful for the forgiveness and second chance he had received. He watched Edwin interact with others, feeling a sense of fulfillment and joy he had once thought lost forever.

As the day progressed, speeches were made, toasts were raised, and the air echoed with the sounds of celebration. Jedidiah took a moment to address the gathered crowd, his voice a blend of humility and pride.

Marshall Thompson warmly shook Jedidiah's hand as he welcomed him back. "Glad to see you made it home safe! You didn't cause too much trouble out there, did you?" he joked.

Jim Davis, the ranch foreman, expressed his relief at having his friend back, which meant he no longer had to shoulder the responsibilities of running the ranch alone.

After greeting everyone individually, Jedidiah turned to face the crowd. "Thank you all for being here today," he began, his voice steady. "This race was about more than just winning; it was about perseverance and the incredible journey we all shared. I couldn't have done it without the support of each and every one of you. This victory belongs to all of us."

The crowd erupted in applause, cheering for Jedidiah and the other racers. The celebration continued into the evening, the ranch alive with the spirit of adventure and the triumph of overcoming great challenges.

As the sun set, casting a warm glow over the gathering, Jedidiah stood with his friends, looking out over the crowd. He felt a deep sense of satisfaction and looked ahead to the future, knowing that whatever challenges awaited, they would face them together.

He glanced over at Agatha Porter and Pat Bennington, two of his loyal workers, admiring postcards he had brought back.

"Oh isn't the Grand Imperial Hotel just grand?" Agatha remarked, pointing at the photo.

"The Grand Imperial Hotel?" Pat Bennington asked, puzzled. "Where's that?"

"In Wichita, you dolt!" Agatha playfully jabbed his shoulder and pointed at the image of the Icarus docked above it. "Don't you recognize Hargrove's ship? This was taken at that convention a few months back."

"Is that the name of the hotel?" Pat leaned back

and chuckled. "Here I was, thinking all this time that it was just called 'the hotel in Wichita'!"

Suddenly, Agatha remembered a package that had arrived for Jedidiah a few days prior. "This came while you were away, Jed," she said, handing it to him. It was wrapped in plain brown paper and tied with twine.

Jedidiah cautiously untied the string and peeled back the paper. Inside was a familiar-looking pocket watch, accompanied by a note that read, "The time has come!" The intricate design of the watch, with its brass casing and green gemstone, immediately brought back memories of the shop in New York.

"This... this is the watch..." Jedidiah exclaimed, his eyes wide with surprise and confusion. "How? Why?" Suddenly, the young ranch owner spotted a logo printed at the top of the note. He quickly reached into his pocket and pulled out the paper dropped by one of the two burly men from the night of the party over two weeks ago. It was an exact match!

As Davenport tried to figure out what it could mean, Phineas clapped a hand on his shoulder. "We're just getting started, my dear boy. The race was just the beginning!" Professor Hargroves didn't realize just how true his statement was.

Jedidiah smiled, renewed determination in his eyes. He carefully pocketed the papers and watch, then raised his glass. "To progress and adventure!"

The adventures of Jedidiah Davenport were far from over. Prepare to embark on another epic journey in *Quest for the Lost Relic* A Jedidiah Davenport Adventure. Join Jedidiah as he delves into a world of hidden treasures and ancient mysteries. What dangers await him? What secrets will he uncover? Discover it all in the next thrilling chapter of Jedidiah's saga!

Current titles in the
Jedidiah Davenport Adventure Series

Coming March 2025
Quest for the Lost Relic